JESSICA BECK
THE DONUT MYSTERIES, BOOK 42
MEASURED MAYHEM

1

JESSICA BECK

The First Time Ever Published!

The 42st Donut Mystery

Jessica Beck is the *New York Times* Bestselling Author of the Donut Mysteries, the Cast Iron Cooking Mysteries, the Classic Diner Mysteries, and the Ghost Cat Cozy Mysteries.

WHEN SUZANNE GETS AN urgent call from her old college roommate, she drops everything and rushes to help her. When she arrives, Suzanne learns that someone may be trying to drive her best friend from school crazy, or worse yet, kill her, and Suzanne must dig into what's really happening. Is her friend just being paranoid, or is there really a target on her back?

JESSICA BECK

To You All, My Dear Readers Who Have Joined Me Along The Way,
And as always and ever, to P & E, Spouse and Daughter,
For taking part in life's journey with me!

Chapter 1

WE WEREN'T EXPECTING to find a body when we walked into the house.

Technically, *Autumn* found it, I should say.

For the first time in my life, I found myself *wishing* that I were the one to stumble across the murder victim instead of her.

It would have made life so much less complicated for Autumn at the beginning, but in the end, I doubt that it would have made all that much of a difference *who* found it.

After all, dead is dead, no matter who stumbles upon it.

And once more, I found myself thrown into the middle of a homicide investigation that could end up being the death of me, or of someone I cared about very deeply.

"Suzanne, it's Autumn," the familiar voice said on the other end of the line when I answered a call at my cottage in April Springs, North Carolina, that I shared with my second—and very best—husband, Jake.

"Not yet it's not," I said automatically. Autumn Gentry (now Autumn Marbury) had been my roommate in college, and while we'd been close at the time, over the years we'd drifted apart until now we shared just birthday and Christmas cards. A phone call from her was rare indeed.

My answer wasn't an attempt to be funny, at least not consciously. When Autumn and I had first met, she'd introduced herself that way, and I'd automatically responded that it was the dead of summer during our freshman orientation tour of the campus, and then I'd told her that I was glad she was getting an education, because things like seasons were important to know out there in the real world. I'd said it all with a grin, and in the end she'd laughed right along with me, and we'd bonded from that very moment with our odd takes on the world around us.

"I know it's been a while since we've spoken last," she said. "I really am sorry I couldn't make it to the ceremony. I would have loved to be there, but I just couldn't make it work. Congratulations again."

I'd invited Autumn more out of a sense of nostalgia than any current feelings I might have had, but I'd still been a little disappointed when she'd failed to show up. "No worries. You sent us a lovely present," I said, remembering the generous check that had helped pay for our honeymoon in Paris.

"Listen, I know this is last minute and everything, but I was wondering if there was any way you could carve out a few days and come see me," she said, her voice taking on a hint of desperation.

"Is something wrong, Autumn?" I asked her.

She hesitated far too long to answer me to be convincing. "No, everything's fine."

"Don't lie to me, girl. We've been through too much together for that, even if it has been a few years since we've seen each other."

Autumn paused again, and then finally, her voice nearly a whisper, she said, "Suzanne, I need you. In fact, you might be the *only* person in the world I can trust right now."

"What's going on?" I asked her. Autumn had been one of the strongest women I'd ever known in my life, even rivaling Momma at times. Hearing the beaten tone in her voice worried me.

"Not over the phone," she said, choking back her emotions. "I know I'm not giving you much information, but if you could come to Cheswick right away, I can cover your losses at Donut Hearts."

The last time I'd seen her in April Springs had been at the grand opening of the donut shop. Autumn had been happy for me at the time, and everyone had loved her instantly. That was just the kind of personality she had. At her wedding a few years later, we really hadn't had that much time to chat one on one, so it had been a while since we'd been able to spend any quality time together.

"There won't be any need to do that," I told her.

The disappointment was real in her voice. In a dead tone of voice, she said, "So you won't come."

"That's not what I meant at all," I quickly explained. "My assistant and her mother would love to fill in for me. Of course I'll come."

"You can say that without even asking them first?" she asked me.

"As a matter of fact, we were talking about it this morning," I said.

"Feel free to bring Jake with you, too," Autumn said a little hesitantly.

"I'll ask him, but it's probably just going to be me, if that's all the same to you. He's helping our mayor remodel his cabin by the lake."

"I thought he was a state police inspector," Autumn said, clearly confused about the situation.

"He was, but he retired. At least he did for a while. It's too complicated to get into over the phone. I'll tell you all about it in a few hours when I see you."

"You're really coming, then?" she asked, and I could hear the slightest spark of hope return to her voice as she said it.

"I'm really coming," I said. Autumn had saved me from more than one jam I'd gotten myself into in college, and if I could repay even some of the interest on her kindnesses in the past, I'd do it without an instant of hesitation. "Are you still living in the mansion on the hill?" It was what we'd called the place her husband had bought for her as a wedding present, a sixteen-room estate nestled in the hills of a small town outside of Asheville's city limits. I couldn't imagine how much it had cost him, but from what Autumn had told me, he'd come from an extremely wealthy family, not that she'd known about any of that until their wedding day. Jeff had managed to keep it a secret from her the entire time they'd been dating, springing it on her *after* they were married. Only then did she learn that he was, in reality, Jefferson Winston Marbury IV, heir to the Marbury fortune. He shouldn't have worried about her motives, even though I couldn't really blame him. Autumn was completely uninterested in money, status, or power.

At least that had been the case when I'd known her in school. Who knew what might have happened in the intervening years?

"No, I'm not there anymore. I've moved out recently," she said, her voice faltering yet again. "I'll text you the directions. Suzanne, don't you have to at least *ask* Jake if it's okay for you to come?" she asked me.

"I'll tell him where I'm going, certainly, but I don't need his permission," I said lightly.

"You haven't changed one bit, have you?" Autumn asked, her voice lightening for a moment.

"I wouldn't say that, but I'm still my own woman. Catching Max cheating on me was one of the low points of my life, but I came back stronger and happier than ever because of it." I lowered my voice a moment. "Is that what happened to you? Did Jeff cheat on you?"

I honestly believed that she was about to answer when I heard her doorbell ring in the background. "That's got to be Lee. I've got to go. See you soon," Autumn said, and then she hung up.

I was sure that I'd get the whole story in a few hours, but it was going to be hard to wait. I couldn't imagine Jeff ever cheating on her. He'd been devoted to her; at least that's what she'd told me the last time we'd spoken.

Had something changed between them, or had something else happened that had clearly thrown her world into a spin? Who was this Lee coming to see her, and had he possibly played a role in what had happened to my former college roommate?

There was no use speculating. I'd know soon enough.

"Jake, do you have a second?" I asked as I walked into the lake house he and George Morris were remodeling.

"Sure, I can take a break," Jake said as he reached for a bottle of water and wiped his brow before taking a drink. "George, Suzanne's here," he called out.

"Hey, Suzanne," the mayor and my dear friend said as he peeked his head out from a doorway. There was a sledgehammer in his hands and a huge grin on his face. Though he was covered with dust from the construction, or destruction, his smile showed that he was having the time of his life. "Jake and I are killing it."

"Just be sure you don't kill each other while you're doing it," I told him. The truth was that it had been some time since I'd last seen our mayor so happy.

"I'm not making any promises," George answered, smiling brightly. "Jake, you've got five minutes, and then I'm going to go ahead without you."

"Got it," my husband said as he turned back to me once the mayor had disappeared outside to the front deck that faced the lake.

"How's it really going?" I asked my husband once we were alone again.

"We're starting to see some real progress," Jake said with a grin. "I'm not sure what I want to do with my life in the long run, but for now, it's fun tearing things up with George. He's good company."

"I'm glad you're enjoying yourself. Jake, I got a call from Autumn Marbury twenty minutes ago. She needs me right away."

"Why, did something happen to her? Can I help in any way? Do you need me to come with you?" I loved that those were the first three questions out of my husband's mouth. He had a wonderful heart, and I cherished it.

"The truth is that she invited you too, but I got the impression that she would rather I come alone. Is that okay with you?"

"It's fine by me," he said. "You don't have to worry about me. Are Emma and Sharon going to run the shop while you're gone?"

"They are. As a matter of fact, I stopped by there first on my way to see you," I said.

"So, your bags are already packed and in the back of your Jeep," Jake answered with a laugh.

"Guilty as charged," I replied with a grin.

"Have a safe trip then, and call me if you need me. Honestly, it's the perfect time for you to go, with me busy here and your mother and Phillip at Duke. If you hear about his surgery before I do, let me know, okay?"

"I will. I still can't believe he didn't want us there with him."

"I completely understand," Jake said after taking another hefty swallow of water. "He's a private man. I bet not five people in the world even know about his cancer. If I were in his shoes, I'd be the exact same way."

"I know," I said. "Momma's going to call me as soon as he gets out of surgery, so I'll let you know the second I find out how it went."

"That's all I ask," Jake said. "Suzanne, if you do decide that you need me, I'm never more than a phone call away."

"I know, and I greatly appreciate that," I said as the screen door opened and the mayor came back inside.

"Time's up," he said as he pointed to his watch. "If you keep goofing off much longer, I'm going to have to dock your pay."

Jake answered, "That's going to be tough, since you're not paying me anything. I volunteered for this, remember?"

"Oh, that's right. In that case, take another two minutes to kiss your wife, and then let's get back to work."

"Yes, sir," Jake said with a grin, adding a mock salute as well.

"I'll call you when I get there," I told Jake.

"I'd give you a big hug and a sloppy kiss, but as you can plainly see, I'm filthy," he said.

"I'll take my chances," I answered as I hugged my husband and then kissed him thoroughly before letting him go.

"See, I warned you. I got you dirty," he said with a grin after we broke the kiss off.

"As far as I'm concerned, it was totally worth it," I replied as I dusted myself off. "Now get back to work before he kills himself without you," I said in a low voice.

"I heard that," George said from the other room.

"Good," I told him, and then I left them to their demolition. "You were meant to."

When I got back into the Jeep and headed west, I had a ninety-minute drive ahead of me, but I was certain it would feel as though it were a lot longer.

There were just too many questions without answers about my old friend dancing through my mind.

Chapter 2

I FAITHFULLY FOLLOWED the directions to Autumn's new place, but as I got closer and closer, I began to wonder if my GPS had somehow made a mistake. This wasn't the high-class district with multimillion-dollar estates where she'd been living before. Instead, there were modest starter homes everywhere. Even those began to thin out as the road got narrower and the pavement got rougher. Finally, I came to the end of the legitimate road, though the GPS urged me on. Then I noticed the beaten-down path through the grass into the woods, so I followed it, more on faith than on assurance that I was still on the right course. A hundred yards later, I was rewarded with the sight of a modest cottage housed in a small clearing, its shingles stained brown, green, and gray with age, the long-weathered horizontal siding matching as well. At least the yard had been recently mowed. There were even some sunflowers planted around the place in different locations. It was what told me that I'd found the right place after all. Autumn loved sunflowers, and Jeff had commissioned fields and fields of them to be planted for her enjoyment soon after they'd married. An old Honda that was beginning to rust sat on the barely graveled path in front of the place, and I wondered just how far from grace my friend had fallen.

A battered old pickup truck was pulling out as I was coming in, and the young man driving it waved to me and smiled as we passed each other. Could that have been the mysterious Lee? He had to barely be in his twenties, with a mop of brown hair and a radiant smile. The guy was handsome, there was no doubt about that, but he had to be at least ten years younger than Autumn, and me too, for that matter.

Before going up and knocking on the door, I phoned Jake to let him know that I'd arrived safely. "I made it, such as it is."

"What's wrong with the mansion?" he asked me.

"Jake, Autumn's living in a cabin in the woods and driving an old car. Something's going on, and I aim to find out what it is."

His voice cautioned me, "Suzanne, be gentle with her. If she's recently split from her husband, she called the right friend to help her through it. I can't imagine *anybody* being better suited to console her than you."

"Thanks," I said as I noticed the front door open and saw Autumn step out. "She's walking out to the Jeep even as we speak. I'll call you later."

"I'll be here," he said.

I had a moment to take in my former roommate as she walked toward me. If I hadn't known better, I never would have believed that Autumn and I were the same age. Not only did she look haggard and worn out, but she had also lost a dangerous amount of weight, at least to my eye. The worst thing of all, though, was the dull and lifeless look in her eyes. Something had clearly beaten this woman down, and for the life of me, I couldn't imagine what could have so completely robbed her of her spirit.

Hopefully I wouldn't have to guess anymore, and soon she'd tell me what was really happening in her life to bring her to the state she was in at the moment.

"Hey, stranger," she said as she hugged me. Again, I could feel the loss of weight in her embrace. Autumn had always been on the lithe side, never seeming to gain an ounce no matter how much she ate, but this woman in my arms was almost emaciated.

"Hey yourself," I said. "You look terrible," I blurted out.

To my surprise, that made her laugh out loud. "I've really missed having you in my life, Suzanne. There's no one else on earth who would say that to me."

"It's out of love. You know that, don't you?"

"Of course I do," she said.

"Was that the mysterious Lee I just saw leaving?" I asked her, carefully watching her reaction.

"Yes, he's been a life-saver since this all started happening," she confessed.

"Is he by any chance the new man in your life?" I asked.

Autumn surprised me by laughing fiercely again. "Lee Graham? No, he's just my handyman. The guy can fix practically anything, and he even mows lawns. Did you honestly think that I'd dumped Jeff for a younger man?"

"Hey, I'm not here to judge. I'm your friend, remember?"

"I remember," she said, growing serious again. "That's why I called you."

As I grabbed my bag from the back of the Jeep, I asked, "Autumn, how long have you been living here?"

"Three weeks," she admitted.

"How did you get sunflowers to grow so quickly in that short amount of time?"

Autumn shrugged. "Leave it to you to notice them. As a matter of fact, I've been planning this move for the past three months. Jeff didn't even know I bought the place. I used the money from my inheritance to buy it after Pawpaw died."

"I'm so sorry," I said. I knew that she and her grandfather had been close, and I hated that he was gone, especially now that she needed him more than ever.

"Thanks. It was sudden, so at least there was that to be thankful for," she said.

"Was it cancer?" I asked, since Phillip's cancer diagnosis had made that my first assumption whenever I heard that someone had passed away.

"No, he had a heart attack after catching the biggest fish of his life off Key West," she said. "The other men in his party said that they'd never seen him that happy. He used to tease me about not wanting to die in bed a feeble old man, and I know in my heart that going out fishing at the age of 87 would have been his first preference if he'd gotten to choose. Anyway, he left me enough to buy this place and live in it pretty much on my own."

"The key phrase in that statement is 'on your own.' What about Jeff?" I asked.

Autumn started to answer, and then she looked around. Chances were good that no one was within a mile of us if I had to make a guess, but she still seemed a bit paranoid talking about it. "Let's go inside. It looks as though it might rain."

There were a few clouds in the sky, but not enough for even a brief shower, at least not in my opinion. Still, I wasn't going to argue with her about it. "I'm right behind you."

We walked up onto the porch, and I saw a pair of friendly rockers sitting there as though they were waiting for us to take advantage of them, light quilts draped over the backs of both of them. A bird feeder hung from one post while a hummingbird feeder hung from another. She saw me checking the feeders out and explained, "I know you're not supposed to keep feeding the birds in the summer, but I find their presence so soothing, don't you?"

"I get it," I said. "This setting feels like home to me; it's so much like where my cottage is positioned."

"Yes, but *you* live near a public park," she said as she looked around the woods surrounding us. "I'm out here all by myself."

"You're not afraid to be so isolated?" I asked her as she held the front door open for me and I stepped inside.

"No. At least this way, if somebody comes after me, I can see them coming."

I shook my head and put my bag down by the front door. "Young lady, I'm not taking another step until you tell me what's going on."

"Suzanne, I think I'm losing my mind. Either that, or somebody is trying to kill me."

Chapter 3

"WHAT'S GOING ON, AUTUMN?" I asked her once we were settled in the cozy living room of the cottage and my bag was in the guest
bedroom. The furniture was all well worn, and a few ragged rugs covered the painted hardwood floors. Everything had faded over time, and
the entire place looked as though it had been transported from the
1940s to the present. Wood covered the ceilings, and the walls had
been plastered and painted a faded shade of blue that reminded me of
old milk paint.

Autumn curled up in her chair, took a deep breath, and then she
began. "I guess the best place to start is the beginning."

She paused again, but I knew better than to push her. She would
take her time telling me what was going on, and now that I was there
with her, I didn't find myself in as much of a hurry as I had been earlier.

"Up until three months ago, if you had asked me if I was happy, I
wouldn't have hesitated to say yes. Jeff was the perfect husband, practically doting on me. But then his brother, Adam, came to town, and
everything suddenly changed."

"I didn't know your husband had a brother," I said.

"Neither did I," Autumn admitted. "He wasn't there during our
courtship *or* the wedding, and Jeff never mentioned him. One day out
of the blue, this stranger just showed up unannounced, and he's been in
Cheswick ever since."

"What's he like?"

"The easiest way to describe him is to say that he's everything Jeff
isn't. My husband is as friendly as a puppy, blond and blue-eyed, but
Adam is dark, and it's not just his hair color or his eyes that I'm talking
about, though that's true enough. The day I met him, I caught him staring at me when he didn't realize I was looking, and there was something about the way he was taking me in that set me on edge. Adam

tried to cover it with a smile when he realized that I'd caught him, but it was cold and completely devoid of any warmth. I said something to Jeff about it later, but he told me that it was all in my imagination. I knew better. Cecile suddenly changed as well when Adam came back to town."

"Your mother-in-law was probably just happy to have both of her sons home again," I said. Cecile Marbury was the matriarch of the clan, and she wanted everyone to know it. She'd struck me as a bit cold during the wedding, but I'd written it off to the fact that her son was getting married, and to a commoner at that.

"That was part of it," Autumn said. "But Cecile seemed to be equal parts angry and afraid, and she started to take it out on me."

"How did she do that?"

"Suddenly *nothing* I did was good enough for her," Autumn explained as she started absently playing with a strand of her hair. "She became critical of my every move, and to make matters worse, Jeff wouldn't stand up for me. When I tried to talk to him about it in private, he just brushed me off."

"So you two started arguing, which led to you being here alone," I said.

"Partly, but it's not that simple," she answered.

"Then explain it to me."

"It didn't help that Adam stayed with us instead of his mother," she went on, deflecting my request for more specific information about her relationship with her husband. "That made Cecile angry, but he wasn't about to change his mind. Adam practically invited himself to move in, and I couldn't very well claim there wasn't any room for him, not in that mausoleum we lived in."

"That must have been tough on you," I said, doing my best to sympathize with her. So far she'd described an unhappy stretch in her marriage, but I hadn't heard anything to make me believe that someone might be trying to kill her.

"It wasn't easy, but soon enough, things started getting worse," she said.

"How so?" Maybe now we would get to the meat of the matter.

"Around that time, I started hearing voices," she said softly, as though she were afraid that someone else might hear her confession.

"Voices?"

"Only at night, always in whispers, when everyone else was asleep," she said. "I woke Jeff up a few times so he could hear them for himself, but they always seemed to stop whenever I tried."

"It was probably just Adam talking to someone on the phone in another part of the house," I suggested.

"I considered that possibility, at least at first, but when the voices woke me again, I decided to investigate. I hated being frightened in my own home!"

"What did you discover?" I asked her.

"Adam wasn't even there, so it couldn't have been him!" she explained. "His car wasn't in the driveway, and his bed hadn't been slept in. There was no way his could have been one of the voices I'd heard."

"Could it have been a television or a radio left on by accident?" I asked.

"No, I searched the place from the attic to the basement. There was nothing."

"How about the wind?" I asked. "Sometimes I can swear I hear things outside our cottage when it's clear that nobody's there."

"There's never been any wind to speak of when it's happened, and unlike this place, there are no trees close to that house, either," she said.

"I can see how that would creep you out, but it wasn't really life threatening, was it?" I asked her, trying not to dismiss her very real angst.

"Of course not. That all came later," she said. Autumn suddenly stood. "Are you hungry? I am suddenly famished. Let's get something to eat."

"I'm fine for the moment," I said. I didn't want to give her a chance to stop telling me what was bothering her, and I was afraid that if she stopped at that moment, it would take her another hour to get back to telling me what was going on.

"Well, *I'm* starving," she said as she headed into the kitchen. "Suzanne, I've *never* known you to turn down a chance to eat."

It was clear that I was going to lose this particular battle, so I decided to go along with her request. Maybe she needed a little more time to collect herself. I would give her a chance to regroup, but soon we were going to get back into the real reason I was there with her. "Okay, I give in. What have we got to eat?" I asked as I joined her.

"I'm not sure," she said with a frown. "I wasn't at all sure that you would come, so I didn't stock up. Then Lee showed up to cut the grass and do a few other things around here, so I never got away. I'm not a very good hostess, am I?" she asked a bit sadly.

I hugged her again. "Just seeing you again is all that I need," I said. "I'm sure we can whip something up between the two of us."

"Just not donuts," she said, showing a brief grin. "I know they are your specialty and all, but the truth is that I never really cared for them."

"That's it," I said with mock disdain. "I'm leaving."

"I guess I could force one down if you made them, just to make you happy," she answered with a hint of playfulness in her voice.

"Don't knock yourself out," I said, smiling in answer to hearing the lightness in her voice, if only for a moment. "I get plenty of opportunities to make donuts when I'm at work."

I was about to start opening pantry doors when the front doorbell rang.

"Did you order takeout, by any chance?" I asked her.

"Do you honestly believe that *anyone* would deliver all the way out here?" she asked me.

"Then let's go see who's at the door. Maybe they brought food," I replied as I reached the front door before she did and threw it open.

A dark, brooding man was standing there, and he looked unhappy to see me the moment our eyes met. "Who are you?" he asked me shortly.

"I'm me," I answered blithely. "Who else could I possibly be?" It was a Winnie-the-Pooh kind of response, but it was really the politest thing I could think to say to him at the time. "You must be Adam."

That took him back even more. "How could you possibly know that?"

"I have the Sight," I said as mysteriously as I could manage.

"Where is Autumn?" he asked me gruffly, clearly tired of me playing games with him.

I was about to tell him she wasn't receiving company at the moment when she stepped into the doorframe beside me. "What do you want, Adam?"

"Jeff is upset about the fight you two had this morning," he said.

"And he sent *you* to fix it?" Autumn asked him pointedly.

"He doesn't even know that I'm here," Adam said. "When are you going to stop this willful, hurtful act and move back home where you belong?"

"Go away, Adam," Autumn said, her voice quivering a bit as she said it.

"I'm not going anywhere," he said defiantly, "at least not until I can talk some sense into you."

I stepped closer to him. "I'm afraid this conversation is over."

"It's over when I say it's over," he replied, doing his best to dismiss me completely.

"Okay, but you'll be talking to the door in a second," I said as I slammed it and dead bolted it before he could try to stop me. I think the man was so shocked that I'd actually do it that he'd been taken by surprise, which had been my intention.

"You shouldn't have done that," Autumn said after I turned to her.

"Did you really want to stand there and let him try to browbeat you into going back home again?" I asked her. "If that's what you want, I'll open the door and butt out."

"All I'm saying is that he's not going to be very happy," Autumn said softly.

"He'll just have to get used to it. The world's full of disappointment," I told her. "He had no right to speak to you that way. Autumn, what happened to you? You used to be the fiercest woman I knew."

"Things change, I guess," she said.

I peeked out the window and saw Adam walk to his Lexus and drive away. "He's gone," I said.

"For now, but I'm sure that he'll be back," she answered.

"Then we'll deal with him when and if that happens. In the meantime, you said you'd feed me, so let's make that happen."

After surveying her refrigerator, freezer, and cabinets, we decided that we should probably go out instead. "We can stock up at the grocery store later, but let's grab a bite first. Do you have anywhere to eat around here that you like?"

"There's a café I go to all of the time, but maybe tonight we'll treat ourselves to a great pizza place not far from here, if you're game."

"You know me. I love pizza," I said as I grabbed my keys and wallet. "Let's go. I'll drive."

"Are you sure? You just came all the way from April Springs," she protested.

"Are you kidding? I *love* tooling around in my Jeep," I said, but there was more to it than that. I was certain that Adam and Jeff and everyone else in town knew Autumn's vehicle, but nobody knew mine. At least that way maybe we'd be able to eat in peace without someone tracking us down so they could continue their onslaught on my dear friend.

Chapter 4

RICKY G'S HAD A WELCOMING atmosphere from the second we walked in the door, a homey décor that said they were more concerned about their food than their furnishings. The smells coming from the kitchen were amazing, and the arched opening overlooking the pizza prep station allowed anyone who wanted to to watch the pizzas as they were being made. Two couples were sitting by the opening at the moment, the men watching raptly as the biggest pizza I'd ever seen in my life was being created. It was the size of the tabletop, and I wondered how many people it would take to actually eat the thing. I was certain the two middle-aged couples weren't going to be able to do it even if they took a few days. We kept walking to another table, and a waitress named Lacey handed us menus. The thin waitress was in her late teens or early twenties, had jet-black hair, and sported heavy eyeliner as well as a few piercings, but under that façade was a young woman with a snarky smile and lively brown eyes.

"We'll have whatever he's making in the kitchen," I said without even glancing at the menu.

"The 32-inch pizza, got it. Will that be for here or to go?" she asked, not missing a beat.

"Suzanne, we couldn't eat that if we had a month," Autumn said, "not even when we were in college."

"I'm kidding, and Lacey knows it," I said with a smile. "I love your name, by the way."

"Thanks, I got it for my birthday," she said, and I knew right away that I'd just met a kindred spirit.

"Does anyone actually *eat* one of those?" I asked softly.

"You don't need to whisper," Lacey said. "The wives aren't all that happy with the order, but both men are acting like teenagers, and it's been a long time since either one of them could say that was true. I don't mind, though. They're fun. I like people who are different, you know?"

"Then you're going to love me," I said as I offered my hand. "I'm Suzanne, and this is Autumn."

"Seriously? I went to school with a girl named Summer."

"I'm from April Springs. Does that get me in the season club?" I asked her.

"What do you think, Autumn? It's your call," Lacey asked with a smile.

"I'll vouch for her," my friend said, offering the slightest of grins.

Sensing Autumn's somber mood, Lacey became all business. "What are we having to drink this evening, ladies?"

"How's your sweet tea?" I asked her.

"Strong enough to walk out of here on its own, and sweet enough to break your heart," she said with a slight smile.

"Sounds good to me," I said.

"Make it two," Autumn said.

Once Lacey returned with our drinks, we were ready to order. I said, "As much as I'd love to try one of those monsters, we'd better stick with a large pepperoni." Autumn had wanted to order a medium, but I was starving, and I wasn't sure when we'd be eating again.

"Sounds good. Salads?"

"No, just the pizza," I said.

"I'll put your order right in," Lacey said, and then she disappeared into the kitchen. I could see that the pizza chef had spread sauce and then cheese on the massive pizza and was now carefully placing enough pepperoni on the top of it to cover most of the cheese. Next came the sausage, the mushrooms, green peppers, and onions. Before he slid it onto its own shelf in the pizza oven, he lifted a corner of the dough and blew under it, forming a bubble in the middle of the massive pizza.

"I really appreciate you coming," Autumn said, and I turned my attention back to her.

"But," I replied.

"No buts."

"Autumn, I'm sorry if I overstepped my bounds with Adam. I just hated seeing him try to bully you like that."

"I appreciate you having my back, but it's almost better than what Jeff does. He's clearly baffled by my behavior, even after what happened three weeks ago."

"What exactly happened?" I asked her.

"Not here," she said in a hushed tone.

"Autumn, absolutely no one in this restaurant is paying any attention to us." It was true enough. There was just one other couple besides the table of four in the restaurant, which didn't surprise me. It was a bit early for most people, but I'd missed my lunch, and I *hated* missing meals. The couples who had clearly ordered the gigantic pizza were oddly silent, with the wives glancing from time to time at their husbands, then looking at each other and shrugging. It was an odd dynamic for sure.

"I just can't," she said, her voice choking a little. "Suzanne, couldn't we just enjoy this for what it is, two old friends getting together who haven't seen each other in a long time? I'm craving something normal in my life right now."

I saw that she was about to crack, so I knew it was time to back off, at least for the moment. "I'll agree to that, as long as you promise that you'll tell me everything when we get back to your place."

"Fine," she said. "How are things in April Springs?"

I couldn't tell her about Phillip. He'd asked me to respect his privacy, and I had every intention of keeping that promise. As I was about to tell her something trivial from my life, my phone rang.

It was Momma.

"I'm sorry, but I have to take this," I said as I stood.

"No worries. I'll be right here," she said.

I stepped outside as I answered the phone. "How is he?"

"The doctor says it went off without a hitch," she said. "My husband is short one prostate, and hopefully they were able to get all of the cancer as well."

"Is there any reason to believe that they didn't?" I asked her.

"No, no one has said anything to the contrary," my mother said. It was the second time that day I'd heard tough women sound defeated, and it rattled me to my core. These were two resilient ladies that epitomized strength to me.

"Momma, you sound tired," I told her.

"I am," she admitted, something that was rare indeed. "He's staying here overnight, and I'm bringing him home tomorrow. I can't believe how quickly they are discharging him, but I don't exactly have a say in the matter. Phillip meant what he said, Suzanne. No party, no fuss. He doesn't even want visitors until he's back on his feet again."

"I understand," I said. "Well, not really, but Jake does, and that's good enough for me. I'm near Asheville right now anyway."

"Why is that?" Momma asked. "Is Jake with you?"

"No, I'm alone," I said. "Autumn called me from Cheswick."

"I'm so glad you two are getting together. How is she?"

"Not great," I admitted.

"What's going on?"

"Don't worry about it, Momma. You have enough to deal with at the moment."

"Nonsense," my mother said. "Frankly, I could use the distraction."

"Her marriage is in trouble, though she hasn't told me why just yet," I said. I couldn't exactly tell Momma that someone was trying to kill Autumn, at least not until I heard the evidence myself. In the meantime, what I'd said was clearly true enough.

"Just be there for her, dear," Momma said. "If there's anything I can do, call me."

"I will," I said, laughing a bit.

"What is so amusing, Suzanne?" Momma asked.

"I've got a feeling you're going to have your hands full with your husband," I said. "I should be home in a few days if you need me."

"Stay as long as you need to. She needs you."

"You might, too," I said, "and mothers trump friends, ten out of ten."

Momma laughed, a sound I never tired of hearing. "If things get dire, I'll let you know. In the meantime, take care of that dear, sweet girl."

Neither Autumn nor I had been dear, sweet girls in a long time, but I didn't contradict her. "I will," I answered.

"I need to go," Momma said. "Will you call Jake for me?"

"I'm on it," I said.

"Thank you. I love you, Suzanne."

"Love you too, Momma."

After calling Jake and giving him the news, I walked back in just as Lacey was carrying the monster pizza out of the kitchen to the spare table they'd set aside by the foursome. It literally filled the entire table when she struggled to put it down, and for a second I was worried she might drop it, but she righted the ship just in time and made it safely to port.

"Enjoy," she said as the men smiled and one of the women groaned. "I told you both before, I can just eat one piece," she told them.

"That's fine," he said. "We can handle it, right, Jim?"

His friend looked at the pizza as though he'd just made the biggest mistake of his life, but he managed a weak smile. "You bet," he said.

They were clearly overmatched.

Lacey grabbed a pitcher of tea and topped off our glasses.

"How much does that thing weigh?" I asked her.

"Fifteen pounds," she said.

"How do you manage to carry it by yourself?" Autumn asked her.

"I'm tougher than I look. Besides, I have the strength of ten because my heart is pure."

I had to laugh. This young lady had a lot going on, and I was going to over-tip her generously to show my approval. "I love a server who quotes Tennyson," I told her.

"What can I say? Nobody's just one thing," she replied with a smile, clearly pleased that I'd recognized the quote from Galahad. "Be back with your pizza soon."

Autumn and I openly stared as the party of four tackled their massive pizza with less and less enthusiasm until one of the men waved his napkin in the air. "I'm through," he said.

The other nodded. "I can eat one more."

His wife shook her head. "Gray, stop. You're going to make yourself sick. We can get the rest to go."

He looked at her for a moment and then threw his napkin down as well after waving it halfheartedly. "It's still going to make a great story, and Jim got lots of pictures."

Our pizza came, and it looked amazing. The crust was one of the best I'd ever had, and I had to wonder what my friends at Napoli's would think. Knowing Angelica, she'd probably waltz right into the kitchen and demand a lesson on the spot. That was the thing about her. She was never too overconfident in her abilities to try to improve, something I loved dearly about her.

I was still savoring the pizza when Lacey came back out of the kitchen with three full-sized pizza boxes. After she loaded the remainder of the mammoth pizza up, the men split the check while the women carried out the evidence of their doomed attempt to tackle the massive pizza, at least in one sitting.

Lacey's smile turned into a frown when she picked up their check. "They stiffed me! Really?" she asked, clearly unhappy about what had occurred.

Just then one of the men walked back in and handed her twenty dollars. "Sorry about that," he said sheepishly. "I was so full I forgot."

"It's all good," Lacey said happily. I wasn't about to leave her a twenty, but I was still planning on tipping her handsomely. Good service wasn't always something I could depend on, and I did my best to reward it whenever I found it.

We managed to polish off all but one piece, but Autumn refused a box for the leftover pizza.

"If she doesn't want it, I'll take it," I said.

"Suzanne, you don't have to eat reheated pizza," she told me.

"I know I don't have to, but this was amazing!" On a whim, I walked over to the pizza chef while Lacey was getting us our box. Grabbing a five from my wallet, I handed it to him. "That pizza was a work of art, sir."

He took the bill gladly while Lacey walked past. "I'd better get more than that, or we're going to have a problem, Ray."

"Don't worry. I've got you covered, too," I said as I handed her a ten in exchange for the box. The tips were going to be close to what the pizza and drinks had cost, but it had been worth it seeing that monster made and delivered to the table.

"Are you ready?" I asked as I returned to Autumn.

"Suzanne, I was going to pay for dinner," she protested.

"You can get the next one," I said.

As we walked out, she asked me, "Are we coming back here again?"

"You never know, but I have a hunch we'll be eating out again while I'm in town," I said.

"Fine by me," she answered.

We were both smiling about the memory of the meal when I noticed someone leaving me a note on my Jeep.

I was afraid someone had hit me when he turned around and I recognized Jeff Marbury, Autumn's estranged husband, standing there looking as though he'd just been caught with his hand in the cookie jar.

Chapter 5

"JEFF, WHAT DO YOU THINK you are doing?" Autumn demanded as she got up in his face.

The suddenness of her verbal assault made him take a step back. "I just wanted to talk to you, honey."

"Don't call me honey," she said fiercely. "How did you even know I was with Suzanne in her Jeep? Strike that. Adam told you, didn't he?"

"Does it really matter? I want you home." The poor guy really did look miserable. The question was, though, was it sincere, or could it all just be an act for my benefit?

"I *am* home," she said. "I told you I wasn't sure what I was going to do. Pushing me isn't going to help."

"I just don't understand. Dr. Morganton says you haven't made it to your last two appointments."

"Why is *she* contacting *you*?" Autumn asked, clearly unhappy with something.

"You gave her permission, remember?"

"Of course I remember. Leave me alone, Jeff."

He took a step back as though she'd physically struck him. "I can't do that. I love you, and I know deep down in my heart that you still love me, too."

"I don't want to talk about it right now," Autumn said, easing her tone of voice a bit. "And even if I did, it certainly wouldn't be here in the parking lot."

"Name the time and the place, and I'll be there," he said earnestly.

"The only thing you should be hearing is not here and not now," she said.

"Okay, I get it. You know where to find me." Almost as an afterthought, he looked in my direction. "Hey, Suzanne."

"Hey," I said as I walked around him and got into the Jeep. Autumn slipped into the passenger seat beside me.

"Where to?" I asked her. Jeff still hadn't moved from his spot.

"Just drive!"

"Yes, ma'am," I said as I started the engine and pulled away, leaving her estranged husband standing there like a lost puppy.

After we'd gone a few blocks, she turned to me and said, "I'm sorry I snapped like that in front of you."

"That's okay. He caught you off guard."

"It was more like an ambush, if you ask me," Autumn said.

"Do you want to go home? Back to your cottage, I mean?" I quickly added. I didn't want to make her think I was encouraging her to do anything but what was in her heart.

"No, we still need groceries. Let's swing by the store and pick up a few things."

"Just tell me where to go," I said.

She directed me to a nearby chain grocery store, and as we walked the aisles, we started collecting enough things to live off for the next few days. There wasn't really a plan, just something to keep us from having to come out again if we didn't want to leave her place.

We were approaching the checkout line when a stylish woman half a dozen years younger than we were approached us. "Autumn, are you okay?" she asked as she touched my friend's arm.

Autumn pulled away instantly at the contact. "I'm perfect, Annie."

The woman looked a bit distressed, though I doubted her sincerity. "I heard about you and Jefferson. I'm so sorry you two split up."

"We aren't divorced. We're just taking a break," Autumn said as I started loading our purchases on the conveyor belt. It was clear she didn't want to be having that particular conversation, and I was going to do everything in my power to get us out of there as quickly as I could manage it.

"Of course you are," the woman said. "You moved out, though. I heard that part right?"

"Yes, that's correct," she said as I handed over my credit card to the cashier. "We've got to run."

"Stay brave," Annie said. The mock look of sympathy dropped when Autumn turned her back, and I could swear that I saw a smug little smile on the woman's face before she realized I was still watching her. It quickly vanished, but it had been too late.

As we walked outside and got into the car, I said, "Wow, she's a real treat."

"You don't know the half of it. She was Jeff's high school sweetheart. Not only is Annie Greenway gorgeous, but her family's loaded, too. Also, Cecile loves her, or at least she used to, which doesn't help matters. Make no mistake about it; Annie is a shark, and she senses that there's blood in the water. When and if I do leave Jeff, she'll be the first one in line to take my place."

"Are you really thinking about divorcing him?" I asked her.

"Honestly, I don't know right now," she said.

I had to ask her something that was burning in my mind. "Autumn, who exactly is Dr. Morganton?"

My former roommate stared out the window for a full minute before she answered, and when she finally did speak, her voice was barely above a whisper. "She's my psychiatrist."

I wasn't sure how to react at first. After all, I knew a great many people who got a lot of benefit from treatment. "How long have you been seeing her?"

"I don't see her anymore," Autumn said briskly.

"Okay, how long *did* you see her?" I asked, pushing her a little harder.

"When I first started hearing the voices," she said, the weariness thick in her voice.

"I'm guessing she didn't help matters, or you'd still be seeing her."

"Suzanne, she wanted to drug me! I don't want to be numb; I want to figure out what's really happening to me. If it's truly in my head, I'll get treatment, but I know, I just know in my heart, that I'm not imagining this. I'll tell you one thing. If I do get help, it won't be from her."

"Why? Is she not very good?" I asked as we neared the cottage.

"People say she is, but she's in the Marburys' back pocket, so who knows? I don't trust her."

"That's reason enough not to see her anymore," I said as I pulled up and parked beside her car. At least no one was waiting for us there. As we grabbed our groceries and that last slice of pizza and headed in, I added, "I've got your back. You know that, right?"

"I do," she said gratefully. "Listen, I know this can't wait, but can we at least put a pin in this for an hour? I'd like not to think about any of this before I tell you the rest of it."

"I can give you that," I said as we carried our things inside. Once we had everything put away, I smiled at her. "How about a game of Scrabble?"

"Do you really want to put yourself through the humiliation of getting destroyed?" she asked me with the whisper of a grin on her lips. We'd loved playing the game while we'd been roommates, and some of my fondest memories of time spent with Autumn had been playing and laughing, making up words and trying to get the other to swallow preposterous definitions. What can I say? We weren't exactly party girls, but we had fun, and that was all that really mattered.

"Bring it on," I said.

"Cribble isn't a word," I said as soon as Autumn made the word using the B in "blast" as her base.

"Sorry, but it really is," she said as she totaled up her points. "That triple word score really helped. Thanks for setting me up."

"Don't write it down yet," I protested. "What's the definition?"

"I ran the jam through the cribble before I canned it," she said. There was a shade of hesitation in her voice as she said it, as though she were making it up on the fly. "It's kind of like a sieve."

"Nice try, but I'm challenging it," I said as I reached for the dictionary.

From the grin on Autumn's face, I knew that I was sunk in an instant, but I looked it up anyway. Slamming the book shut after confirming her definition, I asked her, "How on earth did you know that word?"

"I ran across it a few weeks ago in an old cookbook," she said with a delighted grin. "You know the rules; you lose twenty-five points for the incorrect challenge."

"I remember, but you don't have to sound so pleased about it."

"Sorry, I can't help myself."

"You had me fooled," I said.

"Suzanne, I've learned over the years that one of the best ways to lie is to tell the truth unconvincingly."

"Man, it's scary how good you were at it," I said. "Okay, my turn."

I played the word "kidle" and started adding up my score.

"Challenge," she said.

"Come on, everyone knows what a kidle is," I protested.

"Definition, please."

"I found a kidle at the antique store," I said as resolutely as I could.

"I'm looking it up," she answered.

I'd taken a shot that she wouldn't challenge me so soon after winning one from me, but I was wrong.

After a few moments, she showed me the dictionary. "If you'd only had another D, you'd have been on the money. It's a dam, by the way, though I have to admit that I didn't know that one."

"Just take the points," I said, laughing at my audacity and the speed with which she'd caught me. Tipping my tiles over to concede the game, I added, "I give up. You win."

It was great seeing her again, but we couldn't put it off any longer. It was time to get back to the business at hand.

Chapter 6

"THANKS FOR GIVING ME some time and space to tell you at my own speed," Autumn said as we sat in the living room, enjoying cocoa. I could have used some caffeine myself, since I was planning on staying up well past my normal bedtime, but hot chocolate had been our tradition when we'd been at school, and I couldn't bring myself to refuse when Autumn had suggested it.

"I know it's not easy," I said, "but remember, I'm on your side."

"I never doubted it for one second," she said. "Okay, here goes. After I started hearing the voices, there were two incidents that told me things were escalating. Do you remember the gargoyles on our roof?"

"They're kind of hard to forget, aren't they?" I asked. "You told me they were cut by the same artisans who made the ones at the Biltmore house. Remember that tour we took when you first moved here?" The house, an incredible mansion in the mountains built by the Vanderbilt family in the late 1800s, was a marvel to behold, and we'd taken the tour at Christmas to see the trees scattered throughout the estate. Almost as an afterthought, we'd signed up for the rooftop tour as well, which included close-up views of some of the many gargoyles that surrounded the perimeter. It had turned out to be the highlight of our visit.

"It was amazing. Anyway, I was kneeling in the garden when something made me look up. One of the gargoyles from the roof was hurtling down toward my usual bench not ten feet away from me! At the last second I'd decided to stop and smell a rose when the carved stone beast crashed down and completely destroyed the bench I would have been sitting on if I hadn't hesitated!"

"Did you see anyone on the roof?"

"No, I was so shaken that I screamed and kind of collapsed right there. It took Jeff forever to get to me, and Adam close on his heels.

They each claimed to be busy in other parts of the house at the time, but I had the feeling that it was no accident."

"Why do you say that?"

"Suzanne, what are the odds that a gargoyle would fall from the roof onto my bench at the exact moment I should have been sitting there? None ever fell before, and to my knowledge, none have since. It's hard to believe that it wasn't planned for me."

"Did you call the police?" I asked her. If she was so sure that it was attempted murder, that's what I would have expected her to do.

"I did, against everyone else's wishes, but I had to know. As soon as the police officer showed up, I knew it was a lost cause, though."

"Why is that?"

"It was Craig Pickens. He went to school with Jeff and Adam, and he's done 'favors' for the family ever since he got on the force. There could have been a crowbar up there and he wouldn't have mentioned it. I went up later myself, but I couldn't tell if it had been an accident or if it had been planned. Still, I knew in my heart that it wasn't just a warning. Someone was trying to kill me."

"Is that when you moved out?" I asked her. I was deeply worried about Autumn. The wear on her as she recounted the story was clearly growing, but if I had any chance of helping her, I had to know everything, no matter the cost to her.

"No, it wasn't until I was nearly killed on a hike on the back of our property the next day that I began to realize that I needed to get out."

She didn't add anything to the story, and I really wanted to wait for her to volunteer more about the incident without prodding her. I gave her two minutes, but she still hadn't told me anything new when I finally decided that I had to speak up, or we'd be sitting there all night. "Go on," I prompted her.

"There's an overlook near the edge of the land that has a steep drop into a ravine. I like to lean against the rails and lose myself in my thoughts, and everyone around here knows it. I needed some space, so I hiked out to my favorite spot and started to lean forward, as usual. I've never been afraid of heights, and it was the only way to see the precipitous drop below. Anyway, I started to put a little weight on the railing when it broke free and nearly took me with it! As far as I could figure it, the nuts in back holding the railing in place had to be missing, but the bolts were still there. I double-checked on them before I leaned on it, that's how paranoid I'd gotten. Whoever did it was careful, and if I hadn't been as quick as I am, I would surely be dead now."

"How do you *know* the nuts were missing? Did you go down to check the railing that failed?"

"No, it was too far down in the ravine," she said, "but the wood was in good shape, so how *else* could it have happened?"

"Couldn't they have just loosened on their own?" I asked her.

"Suzanne, don't you believe me?" The panic in her voice was real enough.

"Of course I do, but there might be a more reasonable explanation than attempted murder," I said. "I'm just trying to get to the bottom of this. Is there any chance we could hike out there in the morning so I could check things out for myself? I wouldn't mind going up onto the roof, either."

"You are free to do as you please, but I'm not setting one foot back on that property." She shrugged as she added, "Even if I agreed to go with you, it's all been fixed, so there's nothing to see. As a matter of fact, it was all taken care of so quickly that I couldn't imagine *somebody* didn't know ahead of time that both the railing repair and the gargoyle replacement were going to be needed."

"I'm sure the railing wouldn't be that tough to replace, but there aren't exactly extra gargoyles lying around, are there?"

"You'd be surprised. Cecile found some through her antique dealer years ago and bought half a dozen spares for both homes, just in case."

"Do you suspect she might have been behind this?" I asked her.

"She made my list," Autumn admitted.

"Do you actually have a real list, or is that just a figure of speech?"

"No, I've been writing one since the last event," Autumn said as she reached into a drawer in the end table beside her and pulled out a single sheet of paper.

I studied it after she handed it to me, and in her careful handwriting, I saw her list of suspects.

Jeff

Adam

Cecile

Dr. Morganton

Annie

"Do you have motives for *any* of them?" I asked her as I handed it back to her.

She went down the list. "Jeff might be tired of me, or he might want me dead for the money."

I had to interrupt her. "Money? What are you talking about? When we were in school, you were even more broke than I was."

"I have a million-dollar life insurance policy, and accidental death pays double," she said with a frown.

"Wow, I never want to be worth more to someone dead than alive," I answered without thinking about the ramifications of what I was saying. "Strike that."

"No, it's true enough," I said.

It was time to change the subject. "How about Adam? What possible reason would he have to want to see you dead?"

"Jeff is in charge of the family's finances, and he can't seem to say no to his brother, at least he couldn't until he married me. I've put a stop to Adam raiding the bank accounts, and he's taken issue with it. I have to believe if I'm out of the way, he feels as though he can manipulate Jeff into doing just about anything he wants to."

It was hard to hear, and I was certain it was equally hard to admit, but at least we were getting somewhere. "Surely Cecile can't have a strong enough motive," I said.

"Before Adam came, I would have agreed with you, but she has a blind spot when it comes to her black sheep of a son, and I'm sure he's been poisoning her with lies about me ever since he's been back."

"Do you honestly think the doctor could have a motive?" I asked her.

"No, but the Marburys have something powerful on him, and he might be blackmailed into doing something."

"That leaves Annie Greenway," I said. "I know she's no fan of yours, but why would she want you dead?"

"She's been showing up around the family a lot lately, undermining me every chance she gets and flirting shamelessly with my husband, which Cecile seems to encourage. If anything were to happen to me, I'm certain that she believes she'll be able to slip right into my place."

I thought about everything Autumn had just told me. Looked at one way, it was all possible, but I had to admit that the overwhelming feeling I got was that this all just might be in her head.

"I know what you're thinking," she said. "It sounds crazy, doesn't it?"

"I just wish we had some real proof," I said. "We can't do much about it until we have something a little more concrete."

"Then I don't stand a chance. Whoever is behind this is clearly too good to slip up," Autumn said, sounding defeated by the overwhelming odds against her.

"Don't be so sure about that." I started thinking about her situation. "Is there *anyone* you can trust?"

"Lee Graham," she said quickly. "I met him when he did some work for the family, and we became friends almost immediately."

"He's done things on your home with Jeff, too?" I asked.

"Lots of it," she admitted. "Why?"

"I'm not sure yet, but I need to speak with him. Can you give him a call for me?"

"Sure," she said as she noticed me yawn. "Do you want to wait until tomorrow morning, though? I know your body is on some kind of crazy internal schedule to allow you to get up in the middle of the night to make donuts, so you must be beat."

"I'll be fine," I said. "Besides, I'm not sure this can wait."

"Then I'll see if he's free," she said.

Chapter 7

I wasn't all that surprised when the young handyman showed up fifteen minutes later, given the way Autumn had described his willingness to do just about anything for her. He nodded toward me as Autumn introduced us, but it was clear that he only had eyes for my former roommate. I didn't care how old he was, the man was obviously smitten with her. "Like your Jeep," he said to me before turning back to Autumn. "What's up? It sounded urgent on the phone."

"Actually, it's not. At least I don't think it is. Suzanne wanted to ask you a few questions."

He frowned for a moment when he found out the reason he had been summoned to Autumn's side, and she added, "It would mean a lot to me."

The frown vanished, and a bright smile replaced it instantly. "You know if there's anything I can do for you, I'll do it," he said.

"What do you know about the gargoyle that fell near Autumn, and the railing that suddenly gave way on her?" I asked him pointedly.

Lee scowled for a moment when he heard my questions, and I had to wonder if it was at me or because of what someone had attempted to do to Autumn. "I didn't understand any of it when I heard about it, and I still don't," he said.

"So, you don't think they were both just coincidences either?" I asked. I wanted to know if he'd ever heard strange voices around the estate as well, but first things first.

"I don't see how that's possible," he said. "Have you ever seen a gargoyle up close?"

"We took the Biltmore tour," Autumn said. "It went all across the rooftops, so we got a good look at a bunch of them in college."

"The gargoyles weren't in college; we were," I said with a grin.

"That's what I meant," Autumn said with the tremor of a smile.

"So you know how massive they really are," Lee said. "I can't imagine the circumstances where one would break loose and fall, not even in the middle of a hurricane." He paused a moment before adding, "Well, maybe then, but nothing short of that. Not only are they secure by their weight alone, but they are also bolted in two places on the roof of the Marbury place," he explained.

"Did you get a good look at the pedestal where the one fell from?" I asked. "Had it been tampered with in any way that you could see?"

Lee shook his head. "They wouldn't let me near it. Mrs. Marbury flew some expert in from New York to secure the new one and check the old ones out as well. He claims that he found nothing amiss, but I never got a chance to speak with him myself."

"What did the police say?" I asked.

"You're kidding, right? They sent Craig Pickens out to investigate. What a joke."

"He's not a good cop?" I asked. I knew my husband had told me stories of officers both good and bad in his tenure as a state police investigator. I supposed it was like anything else. I knew there were bad donutmakers out there, too, though I'd never run across one myself.

"He can be, at least when he's not holding out his hand for a 'tip' from the richest folks in town," Lee said. "My older brother knows him pretty well, and one night he and Craig were drinking. Craig told him how there were two sets of laws, one for us commoners and the other for the very rich. He said he wasn't about to turn down what he was offered, and then he suddenly shut up, realizing that he'd probably said too much. After Larry told me about it, I started keeping my ears open, and I found out soon enough that it was true. Unless I miss my guess, Craig never even went up on that roof before he wrote up his report. I don't guess we'll ever know what really happened there."

It was a dead end, and though I was frustrated by it, it wasn't all that unusual for me to run into a stonewall or two along the course of my investigations. "How about the fence?" I asked.

"All I know is that all of the railings around it were fine," Lee said.

"Is there any chance it was an accident that Autumn nearly fell into the ravine?" I asked. My friend had remained remarkably silent during the conversation. I'd asked her to let me handle it, but I hadn't expected that level of passivity on her part. She must have truly been beaten down by current events, maybe even more than I'd realized.

"I wish I could say," Lee answered. "My gut tells me that the nuts that were supposed to be holding that section of railing weren't there, but it might not have been because of malice." He looked at Autumn apologetically. "I'm sorry, I know that's probably not the answer you were hoping for."

"Don't ever apologize for telling the truth," she said, offering him the slightest of smiles.

Lee accepted it and then turned back to me. "The truth is that I didn't install those railings. It could have been deliberate, or a worker could have knocked off early on a Friday afternoon and forgot completely about attaching that particular section."

"Were any others unbolted?" I asked him.

"No. I checked them all along the edge, and the rest of them were fine. I'm just saying that it's *possible* that it was a mistake, and not an attempt on Autumn's life. After all, how could someone possibly know she was going to lean against that exact spot?"

"I've been known to go there in the past when I was troubled," she admitted.

"Can you be certain it was at that exact section, though?" Lee asked her sympathetically.

"Not one hundred percent," she said and then added to me, "Suzanne, aren't you going to ask him about the voices?"

I could tell that it took a great deal out of her asking me that, and Lee looked troubled at the question. "You're hearing voices?"

"It's not like someone's dog is telling me to kill some stranger," Autumn said. It was clear she regretted that choice of words instantly.

"Sometimes at night I swear I can hear people whispering things, but when I check to see who it might be, no one's ever there."

"Are they talking about you?" Lee asked her. I hadn't even thought to ask that. It was an insightful query that might help me, and it just showed me that I wasn't the only one capable of asking just the right question.

Autumn paused just a little too long for my taste, and while I was pretty certain that Lee hadn't caught it, I surely had. "Of course not."

She was lying.

At least some of the voices must have been talking directly about her, and I began to wonder if it were possible that my dear friend might actually be losing her mind after all.

Autumn took Lee's hands in her own, and I could see a reaction in him as though her touch had been electrically charged. "It's very important that you don't tell anyone about this conversation tonight," she said earnestly. "Anyone."

"I'll take it to my grave," he vowed, and I didn't doubt it for one second. Autumn might not be interested in him, but the younger man was surely interested in my friend.

"Hopefully it won't come to that," she tried to say lightly. "We've kept you long enough, Lee. Thanks for coming by."

"Anytime," he said. "Listen, if there's anything I can do, and I mean anything, don't hesitate to ask me, okay?"

"Okay. I promise," Autumn said.

Lee nodded once, and then he left.

"Be careful with him," I told her once Lee was gone.

"Why, don't you trust him?" Autumn asked, clearly shocked by my statement.

"It's not that. I don't have a feel for that one way or the other yet, but there's no doubt about one thing; he's in love with you, Autumn, or at least he thinks he is."

She looked startled. "I told you before. We're just friends, Suzanne."

"Maybe in your mind, but not in his," I said.

"That's just crazy talk," she answered.

All I could do was shrug. There was no point in saying anything else about it. I'd made her aware of the situation, so how she handled it from there on out was entirely up to her. "What else is on tap for tonight?"

"I'm going to read some, but you're going to bed," she said as I yawned in spite of myself. "I know just how late it must feel to you. Suzanne, we'll get a fresh start in the morning, but let's call it a night now."

"I can do that," I said. "I want to touch base with Jake, and then I'll take you up on your offer."

As I started toward the guest room, she said, "Give him my love."

"After I give him mine," I said.

The conversation with my husband was short and sweet. I could hear the exhaustion in his voice as he recapped the day's events after I'd left the two older men at the lake house. "Jake, are you working too hard?"

"Without a doubt," he said, stifling a yawn of his own. "This is a tough gig for a pair of old guys like us."

"Is there any chance you'll take it easier tomorrow?"

"A bit of one, but not much," he answered with a laugh. "Relax, Suzanne. It's good for me. How are things going on your end?"

"Slow but steady," I answered.

"Anything you want to talk about?" he asked me.

"No, not yet. I'm still working on compiling all of the pieces I need to figure out what's really going on here."

"Well, you know where to find me if you need me," he said. "I hate to be the one who cuts this short, but if you don't mind, I'm hitting the hay."

"Sleep well. I love you," I replied.

"I love you, too," he answered before ending the conversation.

I wasn't sure if I'd be able to sleep, but to my surprise, Jake wasn't the only one exhausted by the day's events. Hopefully, tomorrow Autumn and I would uncover something a little more concrete in our investigation.

If we couldn't manage it, I knew that I might not be able to help her after all.

Chapter 8

I WOKE UP AT MY USUAL time, out of force of habit as much as anything else. For most folks it's the middle of the night, but for me it's the start of a new day.

At least it is when I'm going into Donut Hearts to make the goodies I sell.

On the days when I'm off, I've developed a system. Instead of getting up, I lie in bed, close my eyes, and start counting the different kinds of donuts I've made over the years. I tried counting sheep once, but I kept wondering what their names were, why they were there, and where they were going after they left my dreams. Donuts were comfort food for me in many more ways than just eating them. The odd thing was that instead of jumping over a fence like the sheep did, mine leapt through a ribbon of icing and landed on a rack, ready to go into display cases. I'd told Jake about my system once, and he hadn't laughed at me, which was just one more reason I loved being married to the man.

I was just getting into the cream-filled donuts when something brought me out of my impending slumber.

I wasn't sure if it was my imagination or if Autumn had put it in my head, but I could swear that I heard voices coming from just outside the cottage.

I got out of bed and got dressed without any light, something I was used to doing when I was at home. I didn't have anything I could use to defend myself, though. Once I was out in the living room, I thought about opening the fridge door slightly so I could see with the little bit of light, but if anyone was out there, I didn't want to alert them to the fact that I was on to them. Instead, I used my night vision and searched for something, anything in the house that I could use to defend myself in case things got intense. The only thing I could find that remotely resembled a way for me to defend myself was one of Autumn's cast iron frying pans hanging from a hook near the kitchen. It was a large one, and I knew from experience that the heft of it would be perfect for flattening anyone who had the audacity to attack me.

Creeping to the front door, I slowly unlocked it and slid outside after holding my breath for a moment. There was a partial moon out, and since we were in the middle of nowhere, the stars were quite lovely, but that wasn't why I was outside.

Someone was on the porch!

Creeping toward the figure, I was about to swing my frying pan at their head with all my might when I realized that it was just a quilt resting on the back of one of the rocking chairs I'd spotted earlier.

Letting my breath out slowly, I grinned at my reaction despite the danger I'd felt a moment before. At least no one had been out there to witness me nearly decapitating a rocking chair.

And then I heard it again.

It was faint, but I could hear the voices again for a split second. As I stepped off the porch, I lost it completely.

"Who's out there? I'm warning you, I'm armed!" I said loudly, trying to sound as authoritative as I could manage. It wasn't a total lie; I had the frying pan, and if I needed to, I could use it to defend myself.

There wasn't a sound, not a single movement anywhere around the house, at least as far as I could tell.

"This is your last warning," I said sternly. "I won't tell you again." That's when I realized that I hadn't told them to do anything. "Walk slowly up onto the porch and I won't hurt you!"

I was standing far enough away from the front door at that moment that if someone did as I asked and surrendered, I'd be able to see them, but hopefully they wouldn't be able to spot me.

I was gripping the pan so tightly my fingers began to hurt, but I wasn't about to drop my only weapon.

When the front door of the cottage opened, I nearly had a heart attack.

Autumn came outside and flipped on the porch light as she did so. I could see she was wearing a fluffy robe and bunny slippers, and it was clear that I'd woken her up.

"It's just me," I said as I scanned the area surrounding us, just in case I could spot whoever had been talking.

"What are you doing outside?" she asked. "Come in."

I decided to comply with her request. After all, there wasn't much chance that whoever had been out there had stuck around for our little show.

"Why are you carrying my frying pan around in the middle of the night?" she asked me.

"Wait until we get inside," I said as I joined her on the porch and we disappeared into the cottage together. "I thought I heard something."

"Like what?" she asked me sleepily.

"Voices," I admitted.

I was surprised by her instant reaction. "So I'm not crazy after all."

"You might be, but at least you aren't alone if you are," I said.

"I can't tell you what a relief it is to know that I'm not the only one," Autumn said as she slumped down on the couch.

"Don't get too excited," I said. "I'm not one hundred percent sure of what I heard."

"Don't get cold feet on me now, Suzanne," she said worriedly. "I need you to have heard them, too."

"I'm not discounting it," I said. "I just want to dig into it a little."

"Right now? I'm game if you are," she answered as she started to get up.

"No, we need light, and that won't be coming for several hours. Is there any chance you can go back to bed until then?"

"I don't know. Can you?" she asked me.

"I think we should both try," I replied. "One thing is certain; we're not going to sit around waiting for something else to happen. After breakfast, we're going to dive into this thing and get to the bottom of it, one way or the other."

"That sounds like a wonderful plan to me," she said firmly.

"Okay. Then let's try to get a little more rest."

Autumn agreed, and then I watched as she wedged a chair under the front door so that there was no way anyone would be able to open it from the outside. It wasn't a bad idea, but later we were going to take it one step further and get her a bar that went from the doorknob to the floor. It would keep someone from breaking in short of using a battering ram on it, and I had a feeling that we would both sleep better once we had one in place.

I lay there for a few minutes and was about to give up on sleeping any more that night when, much to my surprise, I actually nodded off.

When I woke up again, the sun was just starting to peek through my window. Getting dressed again, I removed the chair Autumn had wedged under the doorknob and stepped outside.

It was a completely different world in the sunshine.

Maybe, if I got lucky, I'd find something that might show that what I'd heard a few hours earlier had really happened and wasn't some kind of hallucination on my part.

That was certainly what I was hoping for.

"What exactly are we looking for?" Autumn asked me as she spotted me peering under the bushes near my bedroom window.

"I'm not sure, but I'll know it when I see it," I said.

"Tell me what we're doing, and I'll help," she said.

I stood and brushed a few leaves from my knees. "I'm trying to find any explanation for what happened this morning that doesn't involve me losing my mind," I said.

"Just like me, you mean?"

"Just the opposite, as a matter of fact. If I can find a reasonable explanation for me hearing voices in the middle of the night, it will go a long way toward clearing you."

"Then by all means, let's keep looking."

We searched for the better part of thirty minutes, but the only thing I found was an area between my bedroom and the porch where the fallen pine needles and oak leaves looked as though they'd been recently disturbed.

Autumn saw what I was looking at and explained, "The birds tear up the undercover to get to the bugs underneath, and the squirrels are constantly searching for acorns. I'm in a pine and oak forest, for goodness' sake."

I dropped the stick I'd been probing the ground with. "Okay, but we can't let this get us down. There's still a lot more digging we can do."

"In the yard?" she asked.

"No, just in general," I said. "I don't know about you, but I'm starving. Should we whip something up for breakfast? I know I'm officially off duty, but I could make us some basic donuts if you could force yourself to choke one or two down."

"Thanks for the offer, but you're on vacation," she said. "I'm not going to have you make donuts for me. How about pancakes?"

"I suppose I could make those," I said a bit reluctantly. After all, turning down fresh homemade donuts from a professional donutmaker could be considered an insult in some circles.

Autumn laughed gently. "I wasn't asking you to *make* me breakfast. The Blue Ridge Café has the best pancakes in the world. Let's go eat in town."

"Sounds good to me," I said. "Should I drive, or would you like to?"

"My town, my wheels," she said with a smile. "You drove all the way here, and last night, too. The least I can do is escort you around town, especially since everyone in the family knows that we're together anyway. So much for the anonymity of your Jeep."

"My transportation is many things, but anonymous it is not," I agreed. "Let's roll."

We got into her car, and she took off down the deserted lane as though she were on rails. "Slow down there, partner. I'm hungry, but I'm not that hungry."

"Sorry," she said as she eased off the speed. "I just like to drive fast."

"I know that. That's why I'm kind of surprised you're driving a secondhand twenty-year-old Honda."

She shrugged. "It was all I could afford after I bought the house."

"I get that," I said. "Is it tough going from having access to all that money to being on a limited budget again? I'm not sure I could do it once I got a taste of how the other half lived."

"What they don't tell you, though, is that money almost always comes with strings," she explained. "I got really tired of being expected to wear the right clothes, go to the right parties, and yes, drive the right vehicles. The greatest thing about Betsy here is that no one in my former circle of wannabe friends would *ever* be seen driving anything like her."

"You call her Betsy?" I asked. Autumn always named her vehicles, a habit I'd picked up from being associated with her.

"Well, the first time I nearly hit a tree out here in her, I said, 'Heavens to Betsy,' and it just kind of stuck."

"Given the circumstances, you could have called her a lot worse," I said.

Autumn patted the cracked dashboard lovingly. "Don't listen to her, girl. She's got a good heart if you dig down deep enough."

"Hey, I resent that," I said.

"Are you saying you *don't* have a good heart at all, no matter how far down you dig?"

"I give up," I said as I laughed lightly. "Betsy, I formally apologize. You're a lovely young lady, and it's an honor to be riding in you."

I could swear that for just a moment, the engine purred a little smoother than it had been before. It had to be my imagination.

Right?

Chapter 9

WE GOT TO THE CAFÉ, but to my surprise, the parking lot was already full. However, a cluster of nine or ten people came out and headed for their cars, so Autumn quickly snagged one of the suddenly available parking spaces. As we made our way in through the front door, a cute, chubby pony-tailed blond teen in faded jeans met us with two menus. Her nametag said that her name was Susan.

"Hey, Autumn," she said, smiling to me as well. "Before you sit down, I need to tell you something."

My former roommate stared quickly around the room, her face suddenly going to an icy shade of pale. "Is Jeff here? Or Adam?"

"No, it's nothing like that," Susan said quickly.

"Then what is it?"

"We're out of a few things until Herbert gets back from the grocery store."

"We can probably work around whatever's unavailable," Autumn said as she reached a table that was currently unoccupied.

"The thing is, we don't have any more eggs or hash browns at the moment," the young girl explained.

I had to grin. "Hang on. Are you telling me that you're trying to run a breakfast menu without eggs? You poor girl. I'm willing to bet people have been losing their minds. Don't you let them get to you."

Susan smiled at me. "I don't know who she is, but I like her," she said.

"Do you have any idea how long Herbert will be?" Autumn asked her.

"Knowing him, I'd say another half hour at least," she answered apologetically. "There are a few things you could order off the lunch menu, if you'd like. Davis over there just got a BLT, and I was tempted to take a bite of it myself before I served it to him."

"I wouldn't have minded," a man who had to be at least ninety said from a nearby table. His picture was in a frame above his spot. "It would have made it a little sweet."

"Behave yourself, or I'll have to do something about it," Susan said with mock severity.

"You can't throw me out," he said as he tapped the photo. "I'm an institution. And besides, you know you love me. How could you help yourself?"

"I wouldn't dream of trying to get rid of you, but you should probably quit flirting with me. I might just call your bluff one of these days."

Davis grinned broadly, showing that more than a few teeth were missing. "Just because there's snow on the roof doesn't mean that there's not still a roaring fire in the hearth."

They both laughed at that as Autumn turned to me. "What do you think?"

"I say you sold me on pancakes, and now that's the only thing I want. If you're game, I'm perfectly happy to hang around until we can get some."

"Then we'll wait," Autumn told the waitress.

"Excellent," Susan said. "Would you like coffee while you wait?"

"Why not?" she asked. "Suzanne?"

"Sounds good to me," I said. I wasn't a huge fan of coffee, but I'd drink it occasionally.

"Your name is Suzanne? That makes us twins, kind of," Susan said with delight.

"I wish," I said with a grin of my own. "I'm afraid I've got more than a few years on you."

"You're still a pup to me, if that counts for anything," Davis chimed in.

"Thank you, kind sir," I answered formally.

"Anytime," he said as he placed a five on the table and stood, albeit with a bit of difficulty. "Susan, as always, it was an honor and a privilege being served by you."

"Right back at you, sweetie," she said as she took the bill and offered him a bright smile.

"What did he order that a five would cover it?" I asked Autumn. That was a fair price for just about anything, but there were two plates on the table, and both of them were empty.

"That wasn't for the bill," Susan said, overhearing my question. "Davis owns this place, so of course he doesn't pay a dime for his food, but he always leaves me a five-dollar bill for a tip, even if he just has a cup of water. Nancy, our manager, told me once that he trades in a hundred-dollar bill and two twenties every month to get it all in five-dollar bills just for the waitresses here."

"How sweet," I said.

"He's a real honey," Susan replied.

After our server filled up two coffee cups for us, I looked around the place. There must have been three dozen paintings on the walls, and there was certainly one unifying theme among them.

They were all of dairy cows, Holsteins, to be specific. "I think Davis has a thing for cows."

Autumn looked around and smiled. "His late wife was an amateur artist. The only thing she found worth painting was a cow, as you can plainly see. I understand his house sports more than he puts up here."

"She must be so proud," I said.

"I heard she was right up until the day she died three years ago."

"It's so sad that he's alone," I said as I saw him tottering down the street through the window.

"I don't know how alone he really is," she said. "From what I've heard, he talks to her every day as though she were right there beside him, and better yet, apparently he pauses in all the right places when she answers him." A bit wistfully she added, "That kind of voice I wouldn't mind hearing at all."

"I'm sorry things have been so rough on you lately," I said.

"It's okay," Autumn said. "Well, really it's not, but with you here, I'm getting a little hope back."

"I can't work miracles; you know that, don't you?"

Her voice lowered again. "Suzanne, I've been reading about you and the murders you've solved in the past. If anyone can help me, it's you."

"Where have you been reading all of that?" I asked, honestly shocked by her statement.

"*The April Springs Sentinel*," she said. "That writer doesn't always come out and say it, but it's pretty clear that you've developed quite a reputation for crime solving over the years."

Great. Ray Blake was the gift that kept on giving. Still, if his stories had led Autumn into calling me for help, I couldn't be all that angry about it. She'd known to seek me out when she'd needed me, and that was really all that counted. "I'm curious about something," I said.

"Ask me anything. My life's an open book to you."

"It's not all that personal, but what made you read that rag of a newspaper in the first place?"

"To keep up with you, of course," she said. "I did a search online years ago for your name, and imagine my surprise when I discovered that you'd developed a rather unique hobby."

"I wouldn't call what I do a hobby," I said.

"Have you ever gotten paid for doing it?" she asked.

"No, not as such," I admitted.

"But you're good at it, and you enjoy the process, or am I missing something?"

"I like helping bring bad guys to justice," I admitted, "and while I'm not nearly the investigator my husband is, I've managed to hold my own a time or two."

"Then you are an amateur sleuth, something that you can be proud of. I just hope there's something here for you to uncover, and that it's not all in my imagination."

"We'll figure this out," I said as I patted her hand lightly.

Just then a heavyset man with a full beard and a large dragon tattooed on his forearm came in, grinning and holding a bag in the air. "Never fear! The cavalry has arrived! It is I, Herbert the Great."

There was a round of cheers from the diners, and Herbert took the opportunity to bow deeply, nearly dropping the dozens and dozens of eggs onto the floor in the process.

"Did you say 'Late'? Maybe you should celebrate a little less and cook a little more," Susan told him.

"Why can't I do both?" he asked her with a grin.

The big man disappeared into the kitchen, and in short order, our breakfast plates arrived.

I took one bite of the small stack of two pancakes that covered its own large plate after I'd slathered on butter and doused them with syrup and smiled. "Wow. These are amazing."

Susan smiled, but then she put a finger to her lips. "Not so loud. We don't want to give Herbert delusions of grandeur."

"At least not any more than he's already got," another diner said, and everyone started laughing.

Herbert poked his head out through the window that separated the kitchen from the rest of us. "What did I miss?"

"A compliment," Susan said, "but I'm not going to tell you who it was from."

"Does it really matter, as long as it is praise?" Herbert asked with a smile before disappearing again.

We were all in a good mood, but why wouldn't we be? The food was excellent, the service was spot on, and everyone in the café felt as though we all shared a bond for riding out the wait for the eggs to arrive.

As we were settling our bill and ready to leave the café, there was only one thing that could possibly spoil our happiness.

Jeff Marbury, Autumn's estranged husband, and his brother, Adam, nearly collided with us as we tried to leave.

"Come on. Really?" Autumn asked. "You two are stalking me now?"

"Get off your pedestal, princess," Adam said. "We came here for breakfast."

"Take it easy, Adam," Jeff said as he turned to his brother. "Autumn isn't at fault here."

"Neither are you," Adam answered, "so stop being a doormat." He was louder than he needed to be in the confined space of the café, and it didn't go unnoticed.

Herbert came out of the kitchen, carrying a meat cleaver. "Is there a problem, folks?"

Jeff was about to say something when Adam intervened. "Go back into the kitchen, Cookie, and leave this to the adults."

That was clearly not the way to approach the short-order cook. He took three steps forward until he was in Adam's face. "You need to go."

"Why would we do that?" Adam asked, stepping back a bit. He was obviously not used to being confronted by the person he was attacking, and it clearly unsettled him.

"Because I said so," Herbert said firmly, patting the back of the cleaver into his other hand.

"I want to see the owner," Adam demanded.

"Sorry. He's not here," Herbert answered.

"Come on, Adam. Let's go," Jeff said as he tugged at his brother's arm.

The aggressive brother put on a show of considering it when Herbert took one more step forward. As Adam turned to go, he looked at us icily. "This isn't over, Autumn."

"Is that a threat?" she asked him.

"No, it's a promise," the brother answered.

That was enough for Herbert. "Okay, I've asked you nicely. Now I'm throwing you out."

That was all that it took.

The brothers left the café quickly, and Autumn turned to Herbert and kissed his cheek lightly, causing the cook to blush. "Thanks for the intention, but next time, I'll fight my own battles, if it's all the same to you. Understand?"

"Yes, ma'am," Herbert said. Autumn had admonished him with kindness, and I wished that I had the same gift for dealing with people that she clearly had.

Once we paid our tab, we were back out onto the street in front of the café again. "What should we do now?" Autumn asked me when I heard someone calling her name.

It was Lee, and he looked a bit agitated as we approached him.

"What just happened?" Lee asked us as he joined us.

"What do you mean?" I asked in return, though I had a hunch what he was talking about.

"I just ran into Jeff and Adam. Your husband looked angry, but I could swear Adam looked scared to death. What did you two do to that man?"

"It wasn't us. It was Herbert," Autumn explained.

After she told him what had happened, he nodded. "Some folks take Herbert's generally genial nature as a sign of softness, but I've seen him get angry twice before in my life, and he almost became unrecognizable." He added softly, "He must really like you."

"I'm sure he was just stepping in to keep peace in the diner," Autumn said.

"I kind of doubt that," Lee said, clearly a little troubled by the thought of having such formidable competition for Autumn's interest.

"What are you up to this morning?" I asked him.

Lee looked downright embarrassed by the question. "I'm doing some work for Mrs. Marbury," he finally admitted. "I had to pick up some stuff at the hardware store, and I'm going back there later."

"Lee, you don't have to apologize to me for that. I know you get a lot of your income from working for the family. What does she have you doing at her house this time?"

"That's the thing," Lee admitted. "It isn't at her place. It's at yours."

"At mine? Why is she having work done there?" Autumn asked him.

I could tell that it pained him to tell her, but he clearly didn't believe that he had any real choice. "I'm supposed to change all of the locks. In a few hours you're going to be locked out of your own house, and there's nothing I can do about it."

Chapter 10

"WE'LL JUST SEE ABOUT that," Autumn said. "Come on, Suzanne. We're going to pay my mother-in-law a little visit."

"She's not at her place," Lee offered. "When I left her a few hours ago, she was at yours."

"Thanks for the tip," Autumn said.

"Listen, you don't need all of this drama in your life. Why don't you let *me* take care of you?" Lee asked. There was a great deal implied with the question, and Autumn knew it.

"You know that I'm still married."

"I don't care," he said.

"Well, I do."

As Autumn drove us to her old home, I asked, "Do you want to talk about it?"

"As a matter of fact, I do not," she answered in such a way that I knew to drop it immediately.

"Are you *sure* you want to do this right now?" I asked her. "You're clearly upset, and I'd hate for you to say anything that you might regret later."

"There's not a chance of that happening," Autumn said. "This has been long overdue ever since Adam came back. Cecile and I are going to have it out once and for all. One way or the other, I'm going to get things settled between us."

"Okay. I've got your back," I said.

"I know you do," she said.

The juxtaposition of the stately manor Autumn had left in order to live in her modest cottage in the woods was pretty dramatic. Everything at the estate was perfect, down to the slightest detail. Towering above the valley, the property took up most of the top of the hill, with panoramic views all around. Acres of grass were meticulously mowed, and the landscaping alone had to cost more than my entire net worth, including the deed to the cottage I shared with Jake. Six massive stone columns held up the front portico, making it look as though it belonged more in Rome than in the mountains of North Carolina. I knew the interior was just as special as the exterior, but there was another difference between this place and Autumn's new cottage, at least if it had stayed the same since the last time I'd seen it. While Autumn had made a home for herself in the woods, a comfortable and cozy place that was warm and welcoming, the house her husband had bought for her resembled a museum more than it did a home to live in and to love in. I supposed that it was a fine enough place to visit, but I couldn't ever imagine actually trying to live there.

"Let's do this," I said as I opened my door.

Autumn put a hand on my arm, stopping me. "Suzanne, do you mind waiting in the car? I know it's a lot to ask, but I need to do this by myself."

"I completely understand," I said as I settled back down into my seat. "I'll just hang around here and wait for you."

"I appreciate that," Autumn said. "I shouldn't be too long. This is probably going to be a pretty short conversation."

"Just yell if you need me," I said.

I watched her walk up to the front door, ring the bell, check the door handle, and then take out her key. Cecile might be changing the locks in an hour, but for now, Autumn could still get into her own home, whether her mother-in-law was in favor of the idea or not.

Autumn glanced back once at me, waved slightly, then took a deep breath and walked inside.

There was nothing I could do for her at the moment, so I took out my cell phone and decided to call Jake.

"How's it going?" I asked him.

"We're getting close to finishing up the demo," Jake answered. Though it was still fairly early in the day, he sounded tired to me.

"You're not working too hard, are you?" I asked him.

"No, I believe that I'm working just the right amount of hard," he said with a gentle laugh.

"I'm serious. You're not twenty years old anymore."

"Suzanne, we both know that I haven't been in my twenties in a very long time."

"It wasn't that long ago," I protested.

"Make up your mind, woman. Am I a young pup or an old goat?"

"Let's say somewhere in between," I answered.

"Are you trying to give me nightmares?" he asked with a laugh. "How are things going there?"

"Tense," I admitted. "Even as we speak, Autumn is inside her former home, having what is probably going to be a heated conversation with her mother-in-law."

"How did you get left out of that particular chat?" Jake asked me.

"It didn't involve me," I said.

"That hasn't necessarily stopped you in the past. Did you offer to bow out, or were you asked to?" Jake probed.

"Okay, she decided it might be better if she went on her own, but I was going to offer anyway," I said. Though that wasn't entirely true, I hoped that I would have, given the chance.

He was about to say something when my phone beeped and I saw that Momma was calling me. "My mother's calling. I've got to go."

"Let me know what happens," he asked.

I switched to Momma's call. "Hey, Momma. How's Phillip doing?"

"He wants to go home," she said.

"I thought that was the plan all along."

"It is, but it's going to take a few hours for the discharge to go through, and he's ready to leave right now. He's threatening to break out of the place if someone doesn't check us out soon."

"Does that mean that he's doing okay?" I asked.

"It's about what we expected. The surgery wasn't a day at the beach. He's tired, sore, and irritable, none of which I can blame him for. Getting old is not for sissies, Suzanne."

"So you've told me," I said. "Give him my love, will you?"

That seemed to touch her heart, and her voice reflected it. "You're a fine daughter, Suzanne. Have I told you that lately?"

"Yes, but I can never hear it enough," I answered. "Keep me posted."

"I will," I said as I heard Phillip yell in the background, "If someone doesn't bring me my pants, and I mean right now, I'm walking out of here in this poor excuse for a hospital gown."

"I've got to go," Momma said, and before I could answer in kind, she hung up.

I got Jake back on the line. "Hey, it's me again."

"Long time no hear," he said. "I was just about ready to get back to work. The mayor's a terrible boss, at least when it comes to construction."

In the background I heard him say, "I heard that!"

"Good," Jake answered with a laugh. "How's Phillip doing?" he asked.

"Tired, sore, and irritated, according to Momma," I replied.

"That sounds about right. Listen, I'd better get back to work. Thanks for calling."

"You bet," I said.

I waited ten more minutes, and finally I couldn't take it a second longer. I left the car and walked up toward the front door.

And that's when I heard Autumn scream.

Chapter 11

"AUTUMN? WHAT'S GOING on? Are you all right?" I asked as I rushed toward the sound. The house was too big to do a quick search, but at least I had the sound of her voice to go by. "Where are you?"

"In the pantry off the kitchen," she said, her voice filled with sobs. "Suzanne, come quick."

The pantry was more like a room of its own, its shelves lined with enough food to see the occupants through the worst of storms, but that wasn't what drew my attention as I burst in.

Autumn was kneeling beside the body of her mother-in-law.

Someone had bludgeoned the matriarch with a heavy marble rolling pin, based on the spread of blood from the back of the woman's head and her inert form.

The worst thing of all was the fact that the rolling pin in question was now firmly gripped in Autumn's right hand.

As I checked the older woman for a pulse I was sure I wasn't going to find, I asked my friend, "Autumn, what happened?"

"I have no idea," she said, staring numbly at the body.

"Why are you holding *that*?" I asked her.

"What? This? It was lying on the floor beside her. I'm not sure why I picked it up." She stared at me a second before adding, "Suzanne, I didn't do this! When I got here, she was already dead."

"You were gone a long time," I reminded her.

"This is a big house," she snapped at me. "It wasn't as though she could answer me when I called out to her."

Not only was there no pulse, but Cecile's skin was cool to the touch. Whoever had killed her had done it well before we'd arrived, no matter how the scene looked at the moment.

"We have to call the police," I said. "And I mean right now."

"Should I put this down?" she asked as she gestured with the rolling pin. "Oh no. My fingerprints are on it now. That was so stupid of me to pick it up." She reached for a nearby dishtowel. "Should I wipe it off?"

"No," I said as I stopped her.

"But they're going to think I did it," she protested as I took the dishtowel, gently removed the murder weapon from her grip, and placed it on the counter.

"There's nothing we can do about that now, but we *can't* wipe it down."

"Why not?" Autumn asked.

"Because yours might not be the only prints on it," I said as calmly as I could muster.

I grabbed my phone and called 9-1-1.

When a young man answered, I said, "I need to speak to your chief of police immediately."

"Is this an emergency?" the man asked.

I glanced at Cecile's body and knew that she was well past the emergency stage, but that didn't mean that I wanted to be transferred to the business desk, either. "Yes. Get him now."

"I'll need some information from you first," the man said officiously.

"Take my advice. Get your chief on the line. You don't want to mess with this," I said.

There must have been something in my voice that told him I wasn't kidding around. The next voice I heard belonged to an older woman. "This is Chief Samantha Seaborne," she said. "What is this about?"

"Cecile Marbury has been murdered at her son Jeff's home. I am here with Autumn Marbury, the deceased's daughter-in-law. Please come quickly."

"Don't touch a thing," she said before starting to hang up.

"I'm afraid it's too late for that," I said quickly.

That got her attention. "Talk to me."

"In her shock, Autumn inadvertently picked up the murder weapon." I hated telling the police chief that before she even got to the scene, but I didn't want her—or her people—to show up and hear it when she arrived at the scene.

Her snort of disgust was obvious. "Then don't touch anything else."

"No, ma'am, we won't," I said.

After the police chief cut me off, I put my phone away. Autumn kept staring at the older woman's body. "They're going to think that I did it." It wasn't a question; it was more a statement of fact.

"We're not going to let that happen, though," I said. "Do you know any good lawyers?"

"What? Why? I already told you that I didn't kill her. Why do I need a lawyer?"

"Trust me, you're going to want someone on your side."

"Tommy Henson is an attorney in the next town over," she said.

"Chunky Tommy from school?" I asked her, incredulous. Tommy had hung around with us every chance he got, having a massive crush on Autumn all four years, not so much for me.

"He's supposed to be really good," she said. "He handles criminal cases, from what I've read in the papers."

"Then call him," I said as I pulled my phone out and handed it to her.

"It's crazy to think that I even need a lawyer," she said.

"Autumn, we're running out of time here. Get him here, and we can discuss why you need him later."

She nodded, called Information, got his number, and then she was quickly connected. Tommy was short and to the point once he found out what was going on. They spoke for less than two minutes before she handed my phone back to me. "He's on his way. In the meantime, he told me not to say a word to the police until he gets here."

"That's good advice," I said.

"Isn't that going to make me look even guiltier?" Autumn asked me.

"Not any more than having your fingerprints on the murder weapon," I said. It was probably a little too harsh, but she needed to realize that this was going to be a difficult and dangerous situation, and she needed to take it seriously.

"Oh, no. What a disaster," she said.

I wanted to disagree with her, but I couldn't. "Don't worry. We'll get through this," I said, though I wasn't entirely sure how we were going to manage that.

Less than six minutes later, the chief of police showed up. We'd left the immediate area where we'd found the body and were now waiting for her in the kitchen. Chief Seaborne led three officers to where we were standing, and after a quick greeting to us both, she and two of the other officers went into the pantry to investigate. It wasn't lost on me that one of them stayed behind with us. The police chief was an older woman sporting a face lined with creases, no doubt from the worries that came with her job. Her dark hair was starting to show streaks of gray, and I liked her for not trying to hide it with dye. There wasn't anything wrong with doing that; I touched mine up every now and then myself, but I had to admire a woman who owned her gray as though it was a badge of honor. The chief wasn't necessarily a handsome woman, but her stature and presence gave her an undeniable air that here was a person of substance, one to be reckoned with.

We were still waiting for her to rejoin us when Tommy Henson showed up. Tommy had been on the chunky side all through college, but since then, he must have lost thirty pounds and had really gotten into shape. In fact, it was almost hard to recognize him at first, but those twinkling blue eyes gave him away. "Tommy, thanks for coming so quickly," I said.

"Suzanne? What are you doing here?" he asked me, clearly caught off guard by my appearance.

"I'm in town visiting Autumn," I said.

"It's Tom now, in case she didn't tell you," he corrected me automatically.

"Tom it is. I'm still Suzanne, by the way."

He shook his head for a moment, dismissing me, and then he turned to Autumn. "I need a retainer. Do you have a dollar on you?"

"No, my billfold is in the car," she said.

"I have one," I said as I dragged one out of my small wallet. "Here you go," I said as I handed it to Tommy, er, Tom. That was going to take some getting used to.

"*She* has to be the one to give it to me," the attorney insisted.

"Fine," I said as I handed the single to Autumn, who in turn gave it to our old friend from college.

He looked relieved to have the transaction completed. "The rest is just formality, but as your official attorney of record, I'm instructing you to refer any and all questions to me."

"I didn't do it, Tom!" Autumn said a bit shrilly. "I don't have anything to hide."

"You're not going to hide anything," he said calmly, "but if you can't do as I'm instructing you to do, you need to find another attorney, and I mean right now. Look at me, Autumn. Does it look like I'm kidding around here?"

Apparently the soft, happy-go-lucky version of the man had died somewhere between school and the present. There was no doubt in my mind that this man, Tom, would indeed walk away if he didn't get what he wanted.

"Okay, sure. I agree," Autumn said.

"Good," Tom said. "Now don't say another word until we're alone, unless it's something like, 'On the advice of counsel, I refuse to answer any questions at this time.'"

"There's something you're forgetting. Suzanne knows everything I do," Autumn protested.

"Maybe so, but she can't be in our discussions." He turned to me. "No offense."

"None taken," I said. I was more than happy to let him step in and take over.

The chief must have heard voices in the other room, because she came out almost as soon as she heard us chatting. "What's going on out here?" she asked, and then she spotted Tom. "Oh, it's you."

"Hello, Chief Seaborne," Tom said. After his display of authority with us, I was finding it easier to call him Tom after all, and I doubted that I'd make that mistake again.

"What are you doing here, Counselor?"

"Autumn and Suzanne are old college friends," he explained. "I'm representing Mrs. Marbury in this matter."

"I'm assuming you're not referring to the late Mrs. Marbury in there," she said as she gestured toward the pantry.

"Mrs. Autumn Marbury," he corrected.

"Fine." Turning to her, Chief Seaborne said, "Tell me what happened."

"Chief, I'd like time to confer with my client before you conduct an official interview," Tom said.

"Why is that? What is it you're not telling me, Mrs. Marbury?" the chief asked her, ignoring the attorney.

Autumn was about to answer when she just shook her head and looked at her attorney. "He told me not to talk to you." It was quite a liberal paraphrasing of what Tom had told her to say, but it would have to be good enough.

"Well, *somebody* needs to tell me what's going on," the chief said. She then turned to me. "How about you? Is he representing you, too?"

"No, I don't have an attorney," I said, "and I don't want one."

"Suzanne, you shouldn't—" Tom started to say, but I cut him off.

I didn't care to hear the end of that particular sentence. "I can take care of myself."

The chief smiled gently, and I wondered if I was perhaps making a mistake by not having Tom represent me, too. I knew firsthand how much trouble I could get into even though I might be completely innocent. Still, the chief had a point. Someone had to tell her *something* if she was going to be able to do her job.

"What happened?" she asked me.

"We came here to talk to Cecile, but when we got to the house, she was already dead. I checked for a pulse myself, but she was cold to the touch. Clearly someone killed her long before we ever got here."

The chief jotted that down in a small notebook she was carrying. "Were you two together from the time you arrived on the scene until the time you found the body?"

If I answered that, I was going to get Autumn in trouble. I knew she hadn't killed her mother-in-law, but it would look bad once the police chief knew what had really happened. "I won't answer that, if it's all the same to you."

"You can't stonewall me like this," she said, letting a little anger slip through. I doubted it was a tactic; I got the impression that she was honestly frustrated by our lack of cooperation.

I just shrugged. I knew that I wasn't under any obligation to answer every question she asked me, especially if it implicated my friend wrongly.

"What about the murder weapon? Whose idea was it to wrap it in a dishtowel?"

"I wanted to preserve any fingerprints that might still be on it. I told you earlier that Autumn picked it up," I said as Tom's face went beet red.

"Suzanne!"

"It's not like they aren't going to find her fingerprints on that rolling pin without me telling them about it," I said. "She was in shock, for goodness' sake! Finding a dead body will do that to you."

"How would you know that?" the chief asked me archly. "Found many dead bodies in the past, have you? What are you, some kind of cop?"

"No, I'm a donutmaker," I confessed, "but I'm married to a former state police investigator named Jake Bishop."

"Did you say Bishop?" she asked, staring at me for a moment as she waited for my answer.

"Yes. Why, do you know him?"

"We've met once or twice," she said as she jotted something else down in her notebook. "Given your marital status to an investigator, I'm surprised you're not being more cooperative with the police."

"Chief, she's told you all that she's going to say at this time," Tom insisted.

"I need a statement from both of them, Counselor."

"And you'll get them," Tom agreed, "but I need an hour with my client."

"How about Mrs. Bishop?" she asked him.

"Actually, it's Hart," I said. "I only take my husband's name for official matters."

"And you don't think murder is official enough for you?" she asked me.

I didn't have an answer for that, so as a change of pace if nothing else, I kept my mouth shut as I came to a decision. I reached back into my wallet and pulled out a twenty, the only other bill I had at the moment. "I'm going to want change from that, Counselor," I said as I handed it to Tom.

He took the bill and stuffed it into his pants pocket. "Chief, I am, at this moment, representing both ladies in this matter. If you'll excuse us, we'll be in touch soon."

"Make it an hour, or I'm going to send my people out looking for you," she said.

"Let's go," Tom told us, ignoring the threat.

As he led us out of what had been Autumn's home until recently, I had to wonder who had taken a rolling pin and ended the matriarch of the clan's life.

At least I was sure it wasn't my friend.

She'd been with me all day, and despite the time we'd been apart, Cecile's body hadn't had time to get that cold if Autumn had been the one to kill her.

At least I didn't think so, an idea that troubled me greatly even as it popped into my head.

Chapter 12

"SUZANNE, WOULD YOU mind waiting out here while I speak with Autumn first?" Tom asked when we arrived at his office. Apparently he'd done rather well for himself since he'd left school. The place was directly across from the courthouse, and if the firm's name was any indication—Strawberry, Hickock, and Henson—he'd already managed to make partner while still in his thirties. The furniture was all rich leather and quarter-sawn oak, and there was a scent of money in the place from the moment we walked in. A stylishly dressed young woman in her twenties sat at the receptionist's desk, but the other office doors were closed.

"Three coffees please, Lila," he told the woman.

"Of course, sir," she said as she excused herself. The three of us were now alone.

"Why can't she come in with me? Suzanne knows everything I do," Autumn protested.

"We weren't together the entire time," I reminded her.

"I was looking for Cecile," she said firmly.

"Autumn," Tom chastised her. "Enough. Inside, please." It wasn't so much a request as it was an order.

"It's okay, Autumn. He wants to make sure our stories are the same without us collaborating on what we're going to say," I explained to her. "Go on. We don't have anything to hide."

"Okay," Autumn agreed.

Tom nodded a quick thank-you to me, and then they disappeared into one of the offices.

I took the coffee from Lila, but I didn't drink it. She knocked then delivered the other two cups inside. I decided to catch Jake up on what was going on, so I took out my cell phone and stepped outside.

"Hey, it's me," I said.

He understood my tone of voice instantly. "What happened?"

"Do you remember how I told you earlier that Autumn was about to confront her mother-in-law?"

"Yes, what happened?" he asked.

"Somebody killed her."

"Autumn?" he asked, his voice full of alarm.

"No, her mother-in-law. Autumn is the one who found her."

"That's not good," Jake said.

"Wait, it gets worse. Cecile was having the locks changed, and we went to confront her. Like I told you before, Autumn insisted on going in alone to speak with the woman in private, and I agreed."

"It's getting worse," Jake said.

"Buckle up, there's more. After a good fifteen minutes, I heard Autumn scream. When I got to the pantry where the sound had come from, I found her hunched over her mother-in-law's body with the murder weapon in her hand."

After a moment's pause, he said softly, "Okay."

"It was a marble rolling pin, and Autumn wanted to wipe it down to get her fingerprints off of it, but I insisted we preserve them in case the murderer's prints were still on it as well. Jake, was that a mistake?"

"From a forensic point of view, it was absolutely the right thing to do."

"How about from a friend's perspective?" I asked.

"Was the body still warm when you got to it? I know the first thing you did was check for a pulse, no matter what the scene looked like."

"She was cold to the touch," I reported. "The woman had been dead at least an hour, in my amateur opinion."

"Suzanne, I'd stack your opinion up against almost anyone else's I know," he said. "Still, she needs a lawyer."

"She's got one. We both do, as a matter of fact," I told him.

"Why do *you* need a lawyer?"

"I wasn't sure what to say without incriminating Autumn," I admitted. "Tom is an old friend of ours from college, and he's the one she called."

"Their relationship is strictly professional though, right?" he asked me delicately. For a man who'd faced down armed criminals in his past life, he could be downright delicate at times.

"Yes. With Tom it is strictly business."

He must have heard something in my tone. "With Tom? Is there someone else?"

"There's a handsome young handyman named Lee who seems to be around quite a bit," I explained. Before Jake could ask, I quickly added, "I don't think there's anything going on between them, but if there were, I doubt Lee would object. He clearly has a crush on her."

"But she hasn't reciprocated it?" Jake asked.

"No. I'm sure of it. Autumn would never cheat on her husband."

"Perhaps the woman you knew in college wouldn't, but who knows about now? People change, Suzanne."

"Not her. Not that way," I said emphatically.

"Okay. Who's investigating the case?"

"It's funny you should ask. The chief of police is a woman named Seaborne."

"I know her. She's good, but better yet, she doesn't rush to judgment. That buys you a little time."

"A little time for what?" I asked him.

"To find out who really killed Cecile Marbury," Jake answered. "I can be there in two hours."

"Hang on a second," I said. "As much as I appreciate the offer, are you sure that's the best course of action to take?"

"What do you mean?"

"I'm just wondering if your presence might be a little intimidating to some of the people who are bound to be suspects. If I ask around myself, with Autumn of course, they might not be on their guard."

"That's true," he said. "Still, I don't like you digging into a murder without me."

"I understand your desire to protect me, believe me, but I think it's better if we keep this under the radar. How long do you think we have to dig into this?"

"If I were to guess, I'd say forty-eight hours at the most, but I'm not sure you can count on having even that much time. The victim was rich and socially prominent, is that correct?"

"Yes on both counts," I said.

"Then the chief will tread carefully, but trust me, she'll be quick and thorough at the same time. I won't come if you don't want me there." Before I could protest, he hastily added, "That's not what I meant. I was talking about in an investigative capacity."

"It's not that I don't want you, and I may have to call and ask you for help later, but let me see what I can come up with first on my own, okay?"

"Okay, but I'm never more than a phone call away," he said.

I was about to say something when Tom poked his head out the door. "Suzanne, I need you in my office right now."

"I've got to go," I said. "I love you."

"Love you, too," he said, and then I hung up.

"That was my husband," I explained as I put my phone away.

"The state police inspector," Tom said knowingly.

"You've heard of Jake?"

"Not just him, but you as well, Suzanne," Tom said as we walked back in. Autumn was sitting out in the reception area now. "We won't be long," he assured her. "Don't go anywhere."

"Where could I possibly go?" she asked, the resignation heavy in her voice.

"What have you heard about me?" I asked Tom as I sat down in the chair across the desk from his. He'd gone to law school at Duke, which was pretty impressive in and of itself. Was it possible that good old Chunky Tommy was more than he appeared to be?

"The donutmaking sleuth? Plenty," he said as he sat behind his desk.

"I'm hardly called that," I said.

"Suzanne, the Internet is full of an amazing amount of information, and disinformation as well, truth be told, but I know enough from what I've read to understand that you're not new to murder investigations."

"I've been involved in a case or two in the past," I allowed. I wasn't about to admit how many murders I'd helped solve.

"Is there any chance you'll stay out of this one and let the police handle it?"

"Not much of a chance, no," I admitted.

He sat back in his chair and let out a puff of air. "I suspected as much."

"What are you doing searching my name online for, anyway?" I asked him.

"I heard a few rumors about you, so I decided to investigate," he admitted. "The law enforcement and legal communities are both full of more gossip than all of the beauty shops in the world."

"She didn't do it, Tom," I told him, wanting to get the subject off me.

"I don't think she's capable of it either, but the women were battling; that is undisputed. The late Mrs. Marbury was there to have the locks changed in Autumn's home! Of course it looks bad."

"I didn't say she wouldn't kill her, I meant that she couldn't," I explained.

"Go on."

"I touched the victim's neck when I checked for a pulse," I admitted. "She was cold to the touch. I think you're going to find that the coroner's report states unequivocally that she'd been dead at least an hour before we got there."

"I doubt they'll be that specific," he told me.

"Maybe not, but she certainly hadn't been killed in the last fifteen minutes," I stated. "You can bet your last paycheck on that."

"Is that how long she was in the house alone, Suzanne?" he asked me gravely.

"About that," I said.

"I need a more precise estimate than that," he said.

"I could tell you that it was thirteen minutes and seven seconds, but if I did, I'd be lying."

"Fifteen minutes it is. Could it have been ten? Or perhaps twenty?"

"No. I spoke with Jake for around three minutes, and then I waited another ten before I went in."

"That's thirteen by my count," he observed.

"Math always was your specialty. You've been there, Tom. It's a big house. It took me two minutes to find her."

"So fifteen seems about right," he explained. "Suzanne, Autumn has been mysterious about what's been going on in her life lately. Do you know *why* she moved out of her home?"

"I'm not sure it's my place to tell you that," I said after a momentary pause.

"I need to know if I'm going to protect her!" he demanded. "Besides, everything you tell me is in confidence."

"Bring her in and let me ask her for her permission," I insisted.

He didn't appear to be happy about me dictating terms to him, but there really wasn't much he could do about it. "Fine," he said as he picked up his phone. "Send her in."

Autumn came in and took the chair beside me.

I said, "He wants to know what's been going on with you, but I wouldn't tell him until I had your okay."

"Is it significant?" she asked me and not Tom.

"I think so," I said.

"Okay," she answered and then settled back into her chair.

"Would you like to step outside again?" Tom asked her with defer-
ence.

"No, I'll stay."

"Very well," Tom replied. "Go on," he instructed me.

In as succinct a manner as possible, I told him everything, from the
voices at night to the gargoyle falling to the fence railing failing, Adam's
reappearance, and Cecile's sudden coldness toward her. Tom took it
all in, and I glanced over at Autumn a time or two and saw that she
was staring blankly at her hands, clasping them, parting them, and then
clasping them again as I spoke.

Once I was finished, Tom nodded and began scribbling things on
his notepad. After staring at it for a few moments, he turned to his com-
puter and began typing at a furious rate. Soon enough, the outer door
opened, and Lila came in carrying two sheets of paper. "Here you are,
sir," she said. As she did, I caught a glimpse of her watching her boss
with guarded affection. Were the two of them an item, or was it just
that Lila wanted them to be? I'd have to ask Tom about it later, but now
was clearly not the time.

"Read these over and sign them if they meet with your approval," he
said as he handed us each a sheet. Mine said neatly and concisely what
I'd told Tom about my own experience at the house and my observa-
tions, particularly the murder victim's apparent cold body temperature.
It said nothing of why I was in town, or Autumn's earlier experiences. In
short, it told only what needed to be told and left the rest out. I could
certainly live with that. I signed and dated mine, and after a moment's
hesitation, I watched as Autumn did the same.

"Very good," he said as he took them from us and rang for Lila
again. "Two copies of each, please."

"Of course, sir," she said.

After she was gone, I raised an eyebrow in Tom's direction, the most subtle inquiry I could make, but if he saw it, he pretended not to notice.

"What's next?" Autumn asked.

"I'm afraid we need to deliver these to Chief Seaborne," he said. "There will be some questions, but I'll be there. Don't answer anything, not even your full name, without looking at me first." He turned to me and added, "That goes for you, too."

"Am I really a suspect?" I asked him.

"No, and if you do as I tell you, you won't be," he answered.

It was a lot to promise, but I decided not to argue the point.

Lila came back in with the copies, and Tom put them into his briefcase. "The police chief's office is not that far. Let's walk over together, shall we?"

"Why not?" I asked as I stood. Autumn continued to sit there, apparently lost in her own thoughts. "Hey, are you coming?" I asked as I gently nudged her shoulder.

"Sorry, I zoned out for a second," she admitted as she stood.

"Try not to do that when you're being interviewed by the police chief," Tom said.

"I'm fine," she said, but there was a deadness in her voice that I didn't like. This wasn't the time to give up; it was the time to dig in and fight.

I just hoped that Autumn had the heart for it.

Chapter 13

"WHY DON'T WE START with these statements?" Tom asked as he handed both papers to the chief of police.

"Are you trying to tell me how to do my job, Counselor?" she asked him archly from across her desk. She'd been on a telephone call when we'd gotten to the station, and the three of us had been asked to wait in the reception area. Whether it was a mind game or she was on legitimate police business I did not know, but I welcomed the time to reflect on what had happened that afternoon. Jake had a high opinion of Chief Seaborne, and I wasn't about to discount that, but I had my doubts. She seemed a little too deliberate for my taste, as though she'd made up her mind about us already.

Now we were in her office, and she took the papers Tom had brought with us without even glancing at them. "It might save us all some time," he said.

"There's certainly a shortage of that at the moment," Chief Seaborne said as she scanned the documents. First she turned to me. "Mrs. Bishop, or Ms. Hart, or whatever you'd like to call yourself, how about waiting out in the reception area for a few minutes?"

"Is that necessary?" I asked her. I gestured to my statement. "I'd be happy to elaborate on that if you'd like me to."

"Don't worry, we'll talk," she said, "but first I want to speak with Mrs. Marbury."

I looked at Tom, who nodded. Autumn didn't seem nearly so sure, but I couldn't do anything about that. "I'll be outside if you need me," I told her.

"Okay," she said shakily. I wanted to stay with her, but I knew that alienating the chief of police even further wouldn't do any of us any good.

I didn't go far, though. Instead of taking my old seat, I leaned against the wall next to the door I'd just come through. I'd been hoping to hear something from the other side, but unfortunately the place had been built a hundred years ago, and it was as solid as a castle.

Three minutes after I'd been exiled, there was a ruckus from the hallway that led to the front desk. I peeked around the door and saw that Jeff and Adam were there making a huge scene, yelling for the chief and even brushing off the family ally, Officer Craig Pickens.

Adam spotted me before I could duck back behind the doorway and started straight for me, with Jeff in tow.

"Where is she, Suzanne?" Adam asked me fiercely.

"Who exactly is the 'she' you're referring to?" I asked as coyly as I could.

"You know I'm talking about Autumn," he snapped. "I want to look the woman who killed our mother in the eye and spit in her face."

"She didn't kill Cecile, Adam," I said as calmly as I could. I looked at Jeff, who appeared to be just as angry as his brother, though not quite as vocal. "Surely you don't believe it, Jeff. She's your wife, for goodness' sake."

"She's not acting like it though, is she?" he asked. "You can't keep protecting her, Suzanne. She's going to have to face us sooner or later."

Adam blew past me and started pounding on the police chief's door. "Get her out here, Seaborne!"

The police chief's door opened, but it wasn't Autumn, or even Tom, who came out. Instead, Chief Seaborne walked out and got within an inch of Adam's face. "You gentlemen are disturbing the peace. I'm trying to make allowances given the fact that your mother just died, but don't push me."

"She didn't just die," Adam snarled at her fiercely. "She was *murdered.*"

"My staff and I are investigating the case," she said. "You need to leave."

"Where exactly are we supposed to go? We can't go back to Jeff's house," Adam said, his voice cracking. It was the first show of loss he'd displayed since barging into the police station. "I suppose we could go to our mother's place."

"Then I'll find you there," she said.

"Not until we see his wife first," Adam said adamantly.

Chief Seaborne seemed to take that in for a moment before responding. "Is that what you want, Jeff?"

"I need to see her, even if she killed my mother," Jeff said coldly.

"She didn't do it!" I said loudly. "I already told you that."

"We're not going to listen to anything you have to say," Adam said as he turned to me dismissively. "Bring her out here, Chief," he demanded yet again.

"I've said my piece. Now go," the chief said.

Adam wasn't about to move, though. It was a stalemate, but I never would have believed how it was resolved. I could hear Tom protesting from the other room, but in a moment, Autumn appeared in the doorway. "Suzanne told you the truth. I'm so sorry, but Cecile was dead when we got there."

"We don't believe you," Adam said. "You two have been fighting like cats and dogs ever since I came back to town! You killed her! Admit it!"

Autumn's gaze shifted to her estranged husband. "Jeff, you believe me, don't you?"

After a long pause, he said brokenly, "Right now I don't know what to believe."

The words nearly knocked Autumn off her feet. "I didn't do it, Jeff," she repeated so softly that I could barely hear her. "You've got to believe me."

"You're a killer, so it's not hard to believe that you're a liar, too," Adam said as he started to lunge for Autumn.

Chief Seaborne must have been ready for it, because she deflected him so quickly and effortlessly that I almost doubted what I'd seen. One moment Adam was lunging at my friend, and the next instant he was on the floor. The chief reached down to help him up, but he brushed her hand away and stood on his own.

"This isn't over," Adam said acidly as he pointed a finger in Autumn's face. "You're not going to get away with it."

"Go to your mother's home, gentlemen," the chief said.

All Autumn could do in response was look at her husband soundlessly. Clearly she was in shock over his refusal to state that he believed her innocent of murder. On the face of it, it wasn't nearly as vicious as his brother's attack, but I knew that it hurt her much more deeply.

"Come on, guys. Let's go," Officer Pickens said as he approached them. "I'll give you a lift."

"We can drive ourselves," Adam protested.

"Then I'll just follow you to make sure you get there safely," he said with a nod of approval from his boss.

I moved over to Autumn. She looked at me, clearly in anguish over what had just happened. "He doesn't believe me."

"It's going to be okay," I said as calmly as I could.

She turned to look at me with dead eyes. "I don't see how."

"Let's get back to it," the chief said once the men were both gone.

At that moment, I was fairly certain that Autumn would have agreed to go skydiving without a parachute if someone had asked her. She meekly walked back into the room, and soon I was by myself again.

But not for long.

Four minutes later, the door opened again and Tom gestured to me as he said, "She's ready for you now."

"You can't leave Autumn out here by herself," I told the attorney as I walked up to him. "I can handle the police chief on my own."

"Fortunately we won't have to find out if that's true or not," Tom said. "She wants to speak with both of you."

"Is there anything else either one of you want to tell me?" the chief asked after we'd gone through what had happened four separate times. We'd been up front and honest with her about everything that had occurred within the confines of what Tom had allowed us to say, but I knew what she was doing. The police chief was trying to trip us up, but that was one of the advantages of telling the truth; it was a lot easier to remember than a web of lies.

Chief Seaborne pushed the statements away from her across the desk as she turned to study us, each in turn. "Half the town wants me to arrest you right now," she told Autumn.

"Chief Seaborne, clearly you can't do your job based on the will of the most vocal minority," Tom said, starting to get worked up.

"Relax, Counselor. I need some time to dig into this. Unless one of you cares to confess and make my life a great deal easier, I'm not ready to arrest anyone yet." The stress she put on the last word was undeniable.

"Does that mean that we're free to go?" I asked her.

"For the moment," the chief said.

As I started to stand, followed quickly by Autumn and Tom, she added, "Don't leave town."

"Were you talking to me?" I asked.

"I'm talking to both of you," she said. "If either one of you try to run, I will hunt you down. That is a promise."

"We didn't do it," I said stiffly. "There's no reason to run."

"Is there anything else, Chief?" Tom asked her officiously.

"You need to hang around, Counselor. There are a few things I want to go over with you."

He turned to us. "Can you two make your way back home, Autumn?" he asked us.

"I'll have one of my people drive them," she said.

"That's okay," Autumn said stiffly. "We'll walk."

We were a good two miles from her cottage, but if Autumn wanted to walk, then we were going to walk.

"I don't mind," the chief insisted.

"I do," Autumn answered.

Chief Seaborne studied her for a few seconds then waved her hand in the air, dismissing us.

Before we knew it, we were both out on the sidewalk, making our way back to Autumn's cottage in the woods on foot.

I just hoped that no one was going to be there waiting for us.

But that was why the police chief had sent one of her men to escort the brothers to their late mother's home.

I just hoped that at least for the moment, our trouble with them was over.

Chapter 14

AS WE STARTED THE LONG walk back to Autumn's place, I decided that it was as good a time as any to get her mind off what had
just happened in the police station. Besides, we were on a tight schedule if we were going to figure out who killed Cecile Marbury before the
police scrutiny got so intense that we wouldn't be free to move around
and ask questions.

"I still can't believe it," Autumn said before I could bring up the
subject of our investigation.

"I know. She was alive this morning, and now she's not, all because
someone wanted her dead," I answered.

Autumn shrugged. "Of course I mean that, too, but I was talking
about Jeff. Did you see the way he looked at me? Suzanne, he thinks it's
possible that I killed his mother!"

"To be fair, Adam was the only one who actually said that," I
replied.

"Jeff didn't deny it though, did he, or even stand up for me! Is this
what my marriage has come to? I don't see any way of us ever coming
back from this."

I had a feeling that it was true, but I wasn't about to pile on and
make her feel even worse. "There's one way you might be able to salvage
your relationship, if that's what you truly want."

"What could I possibly do to make that happen?"

"We could figure out how to solve the murder ourselves before
things get too far out of hand," I told her.

"Is that even possible? I know you've had luck doing it in the past,
but I wouldn't even know where to begin."

"You don't have to know. That's where I come in," I said.

"Okay, I can see that, but before we get started, you need to know
something."

Was this going to be a revelation of something she'd neglected to tell me before about what had happened at the house? "I'm listening."

"I'm not entirely sure that I want to get back together with my husband, but I'd at least like the *opportunity* to try later."

I nodded. "Got it. Is that it?"

"That's all I had to say," she answered.

"Then let's talk about who might have wanted Cecile Marbury dead."

"We're going to have to open up some old wounds, aren't we?" she asked me.

"If it's the only way to get at the truth, then yes, we are. Autumn, you need to realize that there's a good chance we're going to anger some innocent people with our investigation. Are you ready to accept that as a consequence?"

"Are you talking about Jeff?" she asked me as we continued to walk.

"Yes, and every other person we interrogate. This isn't the time to spare anyone's feelings, not even your husband's. I've lost more than one friend myself in the past because of the questions I had to ask."

"I can do it if it's the only way to get the truth," she said.

"Even if it's with Jeff?"

"Suzanne, I'm not sure *how* I feel about him right now, but one thing I do know is that I don't want him to think I could have killed his mother, and apparently the only way I'm going to be able to do that is to help you solve Cecile's murder."

She sounded sure of herself, and I hoped that she would stick with that resolve. It was one thing to say you were going to do something that might be painful to someone else, but it was an entirely different matter actually doing it.

"Okay, let's start with the people in Cecile's life and try to come up with possible motives for them to want to see her dead," I said. I'd nearly added that we had to focus on anyone who stood to gain from her murder, but I decided my word choice had been good enough for the moment.

Before I could bring it up, she did it for me. "We have to start with Jeff, obviously," she said. "Though I don't know what motive he could possibly have to want to see his mother dead."

"Really? I can think of a few," I said cautiously.

Autumn stopped and looked at me oddly. "Seriously? Like what?"

"Before I say another word, I have to warn you that you're not going to like what I've got to say, but is it possible for you to keep an open mind and not comment until we're finished listing our possible suspects?"

"I'll try," she said.

"You need to do more than that," I replied, still standing there on the sidewalk staring at her. Things were about to get touchy, and I didn't want my friend hating me for voicing what law enforcement was already thinking, unless I missed my guess.

"I promise," she added after a few more moments' thought.

"Okay. First there's financial. I'm assuming that he's named in his mother's will."

"Of course he is, but so is Adam," she snapped.

"Don't worry, we'll get to him in a minute," I said.

She took a deep breath and then said, "Go on."

"From the look of things, I'm guessing that she was well off."

"She was loaded," Autumn said. "She tried to use her money like a club to get us to do what she wanted, but we mostly fought her on it. I think Jeff managed to get in and out of the will a dozen times since we got married."

"Seriously?" If it were true, it just might have provided Autumn's estranged husband with motive enough for murder.

"She never meant it," Autumn said. "It was always a power play with that woman, an underlying threat that she could pull the plug financially at any time, but I doubt seriously that she ever followed through with it."

"Well, there's no way we'll be able to find that out, given attorney/client privilege. We might ask Tom if he's heard anything about it later."

"Jeff would *never* kill her for money," Autumn said firmly.

"What about for love?" I asked her.

"What do you mean?" she asked me in return as she stopped in her tracks again. At this rate we'd be lucky to get back to the cottage by nightfall, we were taking so many stops along the way.

"If Cecile pushed him into divorcing you, they could have had an argument. Things could have gotten heated, and in the moment, he might have struck out at her to defend you, and his marriage."

Instead of a quick blanket denial, Autumn hesitated before she answered. "Things *were* a bit rocky between them lately, probably mostly because of me, but also because Adam came back into their lives. Are we *ever* going to get to talk about him?"

I'd covered my two points of possible motive for Jeff, and clearly Autumn was ready to move on. "Okay, let's talk about Adam."

"He's a bad seed, a black sheep if ever there was one," she said. "Not only do I not trust him, but the man gives me the creeps. He finds a way to worm himself into any conversation, and he almost always steers it around to the fact that he deserves a better lot in life than he's gotten."

"Does he ever say anything specific?"

"Despite being Jeff's older brother, he claims that my husband always got the lion's share of attention *and* money from their mother. It's absolutely absurd, since we took hardly anything from Cecile while she was alive, and there is no way that Jeff *ever* got more attention than Adam. Unfortunately, his older brother has a royal family way of looking at life."

"Excuse me?" I asked.

"Those two men were always nothing more than an heir and a spare, at least in Adam's mind. He thought it was his birthright to get the biggest slice of everything, including money and attention. Cecile treated Adam as though he was perfect and Jeff as someone who never measured up, which was just the opposite of the truth, at least as far as I was concerned."

"Is it possible that you're biased towards your husband?" I asked her.

"Of course it is, but I know for a fact that Cecile was financing Adam's partying lifestyle until recently."

"How do you happen to know that?"

"Why do you think he suddenly decided to come back home? She cut off his allowance, so he had no choice. Cecile was finally tired of him mooching off her, and she laid down the law. Either Adam came home and became a real part of the family, or he'd seen his last dime from her while she was alive. That last bit were her words, not mine. I happened to overhear them arguing when he first arrived and I was still living with Jeff. First he tried to ingratiate himself with her, but when that didn't work, he threatened to leave the family forever if she didn't reinstate his allowance. She told him that he'd never leave all that money of his own free will, and the argument escalated from there. The two of them were still arguing when Jeff came in, and the discussion shut down immediately. After that, Cecile started looking troubled around Adam, and I had to wonder if they were still battling about money even up until today."

I shook my head. "Did you tell the police any of this?"

"I didn't think it was my place to say anything," she told me.

"Autumn, they have a right to know. It will give the chief of police someone to focus on besides you."

"Us, you mean," she said.

"Us," I agreed. "At least call Tom and tell him what you overheard."

"When we get back to the cottage, I will," she said. "Anyway, I don't doubt that Cecile left the lion's share of her estate to Adam, despite their arguments. He always was her favorite, and Jeff knew it, which was painful for him."

"So, Adam could have killed their mother for her money, or in anger because she kept refusing to continue to finance his extravagant lifestyle," I said, summing it up.

"When you put it that way, it sounds pretty convincing," Autumn allowed.

"It's still just speculation at this point. Who else do we have to consider?"

"Annie could have done it and tried to frame me," Autumn said softly. "She's obsessed with my husband."

"Just to get Jeff?" I asked. "Wouldn't that be a little extreme?" It sounded crazy to me, but maybe my friend knew more than I did about the situation.

"She's been trying to get rid of me ever since Jeff and I first met," Autumn said. "Until recently, I believe she had a willing ally in Cecile, but they weren't getting along great lately. I had the feeling that Cecile wasn't sure she'd be upgrading daughters-in-law if Annie replaced me."

"We both know that's true enough," I said.

"How can you say that? You don't even know her," Autumn countered.

"I don't have to. I know you," I said. "Speaking of framing someone else for the crime, I suppose we have to consider Lee a suspect."

She looked shocked by the suggestion. "Lee? What motive could he have?"

"Autumn, he had access to the house, and if he could make it seem as though Jeff killed his mother, that would leave you free for the taking, and probably rich as well."

"That is the most ridiculous thing I've ever heard in my life," she said violently, protesting just a little too much for my taste.

"I hate to have to ask you this question, but I don't have much choice. Has *anything* ever happened between you and Lee? Don't lie to me. I need to know the truth, no matter what light it puts you in."

She bit her lower lip for nearly a minute until she finally said, "Maybe."

When she didn't elaborate, I insisted, "You're going to have to tell me more than that."

"Last month he was at the cottage rewiring a switch for me, and as he worked, I caught him looking at me. When I got embarrassed, he said, "You know I'm here for you, no matter what. There's no job I wouldn't do for you.""

"That sounds innocent enough," I said.

"I'm not finished. When I asked him about it, he said that if Jeff weren't in my life, he'd be the first in line to court me. Can you believe he actually said court?"

"What did you say?"

"I didn't know what to say, so I panicked. I tried to make it sound as though he was just joking, and he got the point and played along, but he was serious."

"I thought you told me he was just your handyman," I reminded her.

"That's all that he is. I never lied to you about that," she said.

I decided not to push her on that. "Is there anyone else? Was Cecile dating anyone that you know of?"

"You're kidding, right?" she asked me.

"I know a lot of women her age that lead very active social lives," I said.

"I'm not saying that it's not possible because of her age, I'm referring to her disposition. I can't imagine that there is a man alive who would put up with her."

"You'd be surprised by what I've seen people do for money," I said.

"That's the thing though, isn't it? If she'd recently married someone new, I could see it as a possibility, but what good would it do a secret suitor to kill her before the nuptials?"

"Maybe she pushed him too hard, and he lost sight of his end game," I suggested.

"I suppose it's possible, but I don't know how she'd manage to date anyone, let alone seriously, without me hearing about it. We live in Cheswick, not Asheville. If it was going on, someone would have said something to me about it."

"Okay, we'll put a pin in that line of questioning for now," I said. "Is there anyone else we should consider?"

We were fifteen minutes from her cottage, at least we were if we didn't make any more unscheduled stops along the way. "There might be one man," she said.

"Who am I missing?" I asked her.

"Henry Charleston," she said.

"I've never heard of him," I allowed. "Who is he, and what is, or was, his relationship with Cecile?"

"He handled her investments, and from something Adam said the other day, he's not doing a very good job of it. She's lost far more money than he's comfortable with, and he's been goading his mother into auditing the man's books. From what I've heard, she was starting to waver in her defense of Charleston."

"We need to speak with him, then," I said.

"Do we really? On what pretense would he ever talk to us?"

I wished that I had Grace there with me. She took great joy in taking on other personas for the good of our investigations, but Autumn wasn't like that. "We can say that I'm about to come into a great deal of money and ask him to help me with my investments."

"Is that true? Is your mother well?"

"Momma's fine. I'll be as vague as possible, but I might mention that I could be getting a windfall any day."

"From?" she asked, openly curious.

"Well, before I left home, I got a notice in the mail that I may already be a winner," I said with a grin. "Who knows? Somebody's got to take home the grand prize."

"I don't think I'd mention that part of it to Mr. Charleston if I were you," Autumn said with a quick flash of a smile. It wasn't much, but given the circumstances, I'd take whatever I could get. "So, we need to speak with, in no particular order, Jeff, Adam, Annie, Lee, and Mr. Charleston."

"How on earth are we going to get any of them to talk to us, despite your planned ruse with the investment manager?"

"We'll tailor our story for each suspect," I said.

"I really wish you'd stop referring to Jeff as a suspect," Autumn scolded me as we finally left the pavement and started walking up the grassy path to her place.

"How else should I refer to him?" I asked her.

"My husband," she said.

"Estranged husband," I corrected her.

"Fine. I just can't bear to think of him as being a potential murderer," she said.

"We don't really have any choice," I told her. "After all, *someone* killed your mother-in-law, and they have to pay for what they've done. If it clears you in the process, so be it, but they left that woman's dead body in your home, knowing that there was a chance that *you'd* be the one the police would blame for it. That alone makes it something we need to figure out, and fast."

"Okay," she said finally. "I'm convinced. I still don't know where to start."

As we turned the last corner, it was clear that we weren't going to have to make that decision ourselves.

Lee Graham was sitting on the tailgate of his truck, clearly waiting for us to show up.

Chapter 15

"I JUST HEARD THE NEWS," Lee said as he swung his legs off the tailgate and approached us. "I'm so sorry you had to go through finding her like that, Autumn. What were you doing back at the house, anyway? I thought you told me that you'd never step foot in that place again." There was almost a tone of hurt recrimination in his voice as he said it.

"I had to speak with Cecile," she explained. "I don't really want to talk about it."

I looked at Autumn and frowned, which she caught. "How did you hear about what happened?" I asked him.

"I was at the Blue Ridge Café when Deputy Pickens showed up and told Davis all about it," he explained. "Listen, Suzanne, we need to respect Autumn's wishes. If she doesn't want to talk about it, then she shouldn't have to listen to me, either."

I smiled at him, but I had to force it. Was Autumn going to miss my signal and blow this opportunity? I hoped not.

"You know, maybe it would do me some good to discuss it after all," she said. I offered her a quick smile. She'd caught on after all. "When was the last time you saw her, Lee?"

"Like I told you before, I was over at your old place early this morning."

"What else were you doing there?" Autumn asked. "Besides getting ready to change the locks, I mean."

"This and that; just a bunch of little nitpicky stuff," he said reluctantly. "You know how Mrs. Marbury was. Everything had to be just so. I did my best to look out for you and the way *you* like things to be."

"I appreciate that," Autumn said as she touched his arm lightly for a moment. He looked at her hand on him and then smiled for just a split second. Oh yes, this guy was smitten, there was no doubt about it. The only question was how far would he go to get the fair maiden?

"It was nothing," he said as she pulled her hand back.

"Did that leave the rest of your day free?" I asked him. We didn't have anywhere near an exact time of death, making getting an alibi from anyone problematic, but I wanted to see if he had one ready, just in case he needed it.

"I wish. No, I've got a list a mile long of folks waiting to get work done. Being handy is a lost art these days. I'm never lacking work."

"What exactly did you do?" I asked. "Your line of work fascinates me." When I saw that he was curious why I was so intent on getting an answer, I had to make something up on the spot. "My husband is thinking about becoming a handyman himself," I said. It wasn't a total lie. Jake had mentioned it once in passing, though he'd quickly dismissed it. Still, he *had* thought about it, if only briefly.

"It's good work, but you have to be able to do a lot of things well," Lee said a little proudly. "Take today, for instance. When I left Mrs. Marbury at Autumn's place, I went to Homer Buncombs's and swapped out a kitchen faucet, fixed a patio door that was out of alignment, cleaned his gutters, and swapped the batteries out on all of his smoke detectors."

"Couldn't he have done at least some of that himself?" Autumn asked.

Lee grinned at her. "He could have, but he didn't want to. I'm happy to do whatever people want me to do. I charge by the job, not by the hour, so it doesn't matter to me if they hit me with a bigger list than I was expecting when I show up."

"How long did all of that take?" I asked, trying to nail him down further.

"Not as long as you might think," he said. "I was in and out in 97 minutes. After that, I went to Myra Sedgewick's place. Her washing machine drain line was clogged and started to back up. When I got to the root of the problem, I snaked out a washcloth from the drain. When I asked her about it, she said she was afraid sewer gasses might get into her house, so she'd stuffed it in there herself. She admitted that she must have forgotten about putting it down in there, and I had a devil of a time getting it out. The funny thing was she'd stored some potatoes in the laundry room, and she'd forgotten about them, too. Rotting potatoes smell pretty bad. I found them after I retrieved the sock, but it took me an hour to get that smell out of the space."

"Wow, that sounds like a pain," I said. "What did you do after that?"

"I took an hour off to go fishing out by the lake," he said. "That's another thing I love about my job. I can take off whenever I please, and I don't have to ask anyone else's permission to do it."

"Did you go alone?" Autumn asked. She was picking up on how to confirm alibis, which I liked.

"Just me and nature all around me," he said proudly. "For an hour, I turned off my phone, and I never saw another person until I got to my next job." He added with a grin, "I didn't see any fish, either, but that was almost beside the point."

"How did you get along with Mrs. Marbury?" I asked him. "Did you two ever have any disagreements?"

He shook his head. "No, she wasn't one to believe in debate," he said. "I knew from the get-go that if I was going to work for her, I'd better keep my mouth shut and go about my business. You can ask Autumn. The woman wasn't a big fan of considering someone else's point of view. In fact, there was only one time in my life that I ever talked back to her."

"When was that?" Autumn asked him.

"This morning, when I told her that it was wrong what she was doing to you," he admitted. "I hate the fact that we had harsh words the day she was murdered."

100   JESSICA BECK

"Did anyone else hear you two arguing?" I asked him. That might be the reason he was making such an incriminating confession to us without provocation.

"As a matter of fact, Nancy Betlaw was walking her dog past your old place when it happened," he admitted. "You know what a busybody that woman is. It's probably all over town by now that I was the one who hit her, if Nancy's passion for gossip in the past is any indication."

That explained the admission. "Do you have any idea who might have done it?" I asked him.

"I don't have a clue," he admitted before turning to Autumn. "How's Jeff taking it?"

"He thinks that I might have done it," she said.

"Hang on. That's not completely fair," I said. "Adam said that, not Jeff."

"He didn't stand up for me though, did he?" Autumn asked, clearly still distraught about what had happened earlier.

"I can't believe it," Lee said. "I can't even begin to *imagine* the circumstances that I would ever do that to you." He looked at her meaningfully, and I had to wonder for a moment if he'd forgotten that I was even there. "Autumn, what I said before goes double. If you need me, and I mean for anything, I'm just a phone call away."

As he said it, his phone rang, an eerie ringtone that reminded me of a fifties science fiction film. He glanced at it, and then he looked at Autumn. "It's Jeff."

"Go on. Take it," she said.

"No, I'll call him back later," Lee said as he started to hit Ignore on his phone.

"He might need you, too," I said, urging him.

"Please, do it for me," Autumn added, picking up on my desire to hear what her estranged husband wanted from the handyman.

"Hey. Yes. No. Really? Hang on." He put the phone against his chest and looked at Autumn. "He wants the locks changed right now, at your place and at his mother's house, too. He offered to pay me triple what I usually charge if I'll do it right now."

"You should take the job," Autumn urged him.

"I don't know. I don't feel right about it," Lee protested.

"The truth is that I don't care anymore," my friend said. Whether she was talking about the new locks or her husband I did not know, and clearly neither did Lee.

"I've got four jobs ahead of you, and I'm probably going to lose business if I drop everything for you. I'll do it for four times my normal bill, but I'll need an extra hundred bucks to make the risk of losing some of my clients worth it."

He paused a moment, and then grinned. "Okay then. Fair enough. See you in twenty minutes. Oh, and that quote was just for the labor. You'll have to pay for new locksets, too." After a pause, he said, "Then we're all good. See you soon."

"Wow, you really gouged him, didn't you?" I asked him, wanting to get a reaction to how he really felt about Jeff.

"I know the man just lost his mother, but what he's done to Autumn is unforgivable. Besides, he didn't have to agree to any of it. If he wants to make it happen, he's going to have to pay for the privilege." Realizing that the transaction hadn't cast him in the best of lights, he added, "I'll make a nice donation to the animal shelter when I get the money. I won't profit *too* much from it, but it's only right that he has to pay for what he's done."

"Are you saying that you think that Jeff might have killed his mother?" I asked him.

"I'm not saying anything," Lee quickly corrected me. "I just don't think he should get away with treating Autumn the way he has lately. Ever since Adam came back into town, Jeff and Mrs. Marbury have been acting pretty odd as far as I'm concerned. I don't think Jeff did it, but I wouldn't put it past his brother."

"Why do you say that?" I asked.

"Just a feeling, I guess," he said. "Listen, I've got to run." As he started for his truck, he turned back to Autumn. "Remember, call me if you need me."

"Thanks, I will."

After he drove away, Autumn said, "At least we can strike one name off our list."

"Really?" I asked as we walked up onto the porch and into the cottage. "Whose name might that be?"

"Lee's, of course," she said, acting surprised by my question.

"How do you figure that?"

"His time was accounted for," she replied.

"First off, that body was cold when we found it, so it's hard to say how long she'd been dead, and second of all, he admitted that they argued this morning in public, and that there was an entire hour that he couldn't account for."

"When he was fishing?" she asked me.

"He told us himself that he didn't see a soul, so how do we know he was even at the lake?" I hesitated a moment and then added, "Autumn, that man has got it bad for you."

"Maybe," she finally admitted, "but I can't imagine him killing Cecile. If Jeff had died, it might be possible, but why kill his mother?"

"I can think of a few reasons. Maybe he was tired of hearing her badmouth you and he lost his temper. Then again, if he could get rid of Cecile and frame Jeff for it, there would be no one to stand in his way."

"But he didn't frame Jeff," Autumn pointed out.

"Not yet, at any rate," I said. "In the meantime, we need to keep digging."

"This is exhausting, Suzanne. I don't know how you do it."

"You could always just stay here," I offered.

"No, this is my mess, and I'm going to help you clean it up. Who's next?"

"I'd like to speak with Jeff and Adam, but they're going to be tied up with Lee for the next hour or two. That leaves us with Annie and Mr. Charleston. Any preferences?"

"I suppose it needs to be Annie," she said reluctantly.

"Really? I thought you'd want to tackle her last."

"I do. That's why we need to track her down next. The sooner we get that interview over, the better as far as I'm concerned."

"Then let's go see if we can find your former rival for your husband's affections."

Autumn glanced at her watch. "Luckily, I know right where she'll be."

Chapter 16

THE SIGN ABOVE THE upscale boutique said simply, PLAT-INUM. I glanced in the window, but I didn't see anything even remotely made of the precious metal. I knew she'd been trying to sound rich and exclusive with her name choice, but would it have killed her to put a bracelet or some small trinket in the window?

I was about to say as much to Autumn when I glanced over at my friend. She was visibly shaking at the very thought of going into the shop. "Hey, are you okay?"

"That woman seems to know exactly what to say to hurt me the deepest," Autumn said. "I'm not sure I'm up for this."

"I can do it alone if you'd like," I offered.

I thought for a moment she might just take me up on it when she shook her head suddenly. "No, I'm fine. Let's go in."

"I really don't mind," I said as Autumn brushed past me and opened the door.

I had no choice at that point.

I followed her in.

Annie Greenway was helping an older woman dressed much like Gabby Williams did, the owner of ReNEWed back in April Springs. The only difference was that I was certain that this woman had paid full retail for her outfit, whereas Gabby only culled the best from her inventory of previously gently used stylish clothing that came into her shop.

Annie glanced up at us as she said, "I'll be with you..." Then she noticed Autumn was there, and she shut down midsentence.

"That's okay. We can wait," I said as I started looking through the clothes for sale. I was fairly certain that I was the first woman in blue jeans and a T-shirt to ever browse in Platinum. I found a blouse that was kind of cute and pulled it out just for fun.

The price tag was three figures, and that was before the decimal point. "Check this out," I told Autumn as I showed her what I'd discovered.

"It would look cute on you," Autumn said, studiously avoiding Annie.

In a lower voice, I said, "I'm talking about the price."

"Well, look at the label. It's worth every penny."

"If you happen to have that many pennies available to you for a blouse," I said with disdain. "Have you ever bought anything this expensive? My first car didn't cost this much."

"Jeff bought me a few things from here," she admitted.

"Okay," I said, putting the blouse back on the rack. I was afraid at that point of even touching it. I glanced back to find Annie ringing up a sale for the woman in question, so she should be finished soon. I didn't want to confront her in front of one of her customers. After all, we might be different in just about every way imaginable, but we were still women running small businesses, and there was an underlying loyalty there for me, even if wasn't reciprocated. "See anything you like?"

"I'm not here to shop," Autumn said tersely.

"You didn't have to come in at all," I reminded her.

"I'm sorry I snapped," Autumn said in a quick apology.

I touched her arm lightly. "Hey, if this didn't have you on edge, I'd really be worried about you."

"Good-bye, Hennie," Annie said as she held the door open for the older woman. "See you soon."

"Good-bye, dear. Until tomorrow."

Once she was gone, Annie turned to us. "I'm guessing you two aren't here on a shopping expedition."

"Does she really come in every day?" I asked as Hennie walked down the street outside the shop window. "She must spend a fortune over the course of a year."

"She can afford it," Annie said. "What do you want, Autumn? I'm surprised you have the nerve to show your face around here after what you did."

"What exactly is that?" Autumn asked her pointedly. She'd been cowed before outside, but now my friend was finding her spine again.

"Come on. Who are we kidding? Everyone knew how you felt about Cecile."

"She was my mother-in-law," Autumn said.

"Not for very much longer," Annie cracked. "Jeff is never going to want you back now, and the sooner you face that fact, the better it will be for everyone concerned."

Autumn stood there, shocked by the onslaught, so there was no way that I was going to stand by and watch it happen. "Do you honestly think he'll come running to you, even if they get divorced?"

"Who are you?" she asked me as she barely glanced in my direction.

"I'm Autumn's friend, that's who I am," I said.

"And what is it that you do?" she asked as her gaze swept from my tennis shoes to my top.

"I'm a donutmaker. I run a small business just like you do."

Annie's laugh had no humor or warmth in it whatsoever. "I can assure you that what you do is *nothing* like what I do." So much for the sisterhood of women small business owners. "Autumn, you need to leave."

"Not until we have a little chat first," Autumn said. "When was the last time you spoke with Cecile?"

"That's none of your business," Annie said, but I saw her cheeks flush at the statement. Was it possible that she really was that agitated, or had we struck a nerve? "Why aren't you in jail?"

"Because *I* didn't kill her," Autumn said firmly. "Can you say the same?"

"Get out of my shop, you murderer!" Annie said shrilly, pointing to the door.

I might not have escalated the conversation so quickly until we could at least get an alibi from her, but clearly Autumn had decided to go another route. She said firmly, "Sorry, but we're not going anywhere."

"Then I'm calling the police. I have the right to refuse service to anyone I choose," she said as she reached for her phone.

"Come on, Autumn," I said as I tugged at her arm. "We need to go."

"Listen to your friend," Annie said, her finger poised to dial the police.

"Fine, but this isn't over," Autumn told her. Before she walked out the door though, she stopped and said, "There's something you really need to understand, Annie. Jeff will *never* love you, even if we split up. You're old news, ancient history, damaged goods."

It was clearly Annie's turn to be shocked into silence, so I grabbed Autumn's arm and pulled her out onto the sidewalk.

"Wow, that was really brutal," I said once we were outside.

"Was it too much?" Autumn asked. "I couldn't seem to stop myself."

"You just returned her fire," I assured her. "She started it, but you finished it. Why did you call her damaged goods? That really seemed to hit home."

"A long time ago, she was married to Jeff's third cousin for about three weeks. They got an annulment, and no one really knows what happened between them, but the rumors are pretty crazy."

"Do *you* know what really happened?" I asked her.

"No. That was probably a low blow adding that. Do you think I should apologize, at least for that crack?"

"I think we'd both be better off if we steered clear of her for a while to give her some time to cool off," I said.

"So, where does that leave us?" she asked me.

"We need to call Mr. Charleston and make that appointment."

"Are you sure you want to stick with the story that you're about to come into money?" Autumn asked me.

"I've got a feeling that it's the only sure way we'll get in to see him," I said.

"Then make the call."

After dodging first a receptionist and then a secretary, I was finally speaking to the man himself. "Ms. Hart, how may I be of service to you?"

"I need some financial advice. You see, I am about to come into a large sum of money, and I'm not at all sure what to do with it. I don't have a very good head when it comes to money, so I'm hoping you can take it all over and have complete control of it for me."

"You've come to the right man," he said. I could almost hear him licking his lips after hearing my admission. "I have a tight schedule, but I can make room for you sometime late next week."

"Oh dear," I said. "I'm afraid I'll need advice faster than that. Never mind, then," I said.

I could see Autumn's concerned look, but I had a feeling it was the right move. I'd put the phone up so she could hear both sides of the conversation.

He barely hesitated in his response. "Well, you're in luck. It seems I've had a cancellation at seven this evening. I'd be happy to come by your home and discuss this with you in person."

"Oh, I don't take meetings at home. It's a bit too intimate," I said quickly. "Your office?"

"Of course," he said, though it was clear he wasn't thrilled with my demand. He probably wanted to size up my net worth by seeing what was around me, and I couldn't have that. As it was, I was going to have to do some tap dancing to convince him that I was legitimate. "I'm afraid I have to insist on knowing the source of your windfall before we meet, though. It's a matter of structuring your portfolio properly."

"Is that absolutely necessary?" I asked him. Suddenly my "check is in the mail" story wasn't going to work.

"I'm afraid so, yes," he said.

"My mother is about to bestow a rather large gift of cash and stocks to me," I said in a panic, not knowing what else to say.

"Very well. Her name?"

"Dorothea Hart," I said. After all, in for a penny, in for a pound.

"Very well. I'll see you at seven."

The moment we hung up, Autumn started in on me. "Suzanne, that wasn't going to be your story at all. Why did you tell him that? He can check her out."

I held up one hand. "One second." I dialed Momma's number, and to my relief, she picked up right away.

"Hello, Suzanne. Phillip's fine. Thanks for calling."

"I'm glad," I said. "Listen, a man named Henry Charleston might call you to find out if you're giving me a great deal of money very soon."

She didn't even hesitate. "Suzanne, are you in some kind of trouble?"

"Relax, Momma. You don't have to actually *give* me any cash, but if he calls, tell him that you're about to."

"What is this about?"

"I don't have a lot of time for questions," I said.

"Then I won't ask any more. Go on. I'm listening."

I knew I had no choice but to admit what was really going on. "Somebody killed Autumn's mother-in-law, and the police suspect her. We're trying to clear her name, and Charleston was the victim's financial planner. In order to secure an appointment with him, I have to prove that I'm going to be getting enough from you to make it worth his while."

Say what you wanted to about my mother, but she was extremely quick on the uptake. "How does three million dollars sound to you?"

The number caught me by surprise. "Momma, just how rich *are* you?"

She chuckled before responding, "Rich enough."

In the background, I heard Phillip call out, "Dot, I need you."

"I've got to go," Momma said. "Be safe, child."

"Thanks, Momma."

"Of course."

Now it was a matter of waiting until it was time to meet with Mr. Charleston to see what we could uncover about his relationship with the late Mrs. Marbury.

We were down to the last two names on our list, the brothers Marbury: Jeff and Adam.

I knew these would be the hardest interviews for us to conduct, but it was no longer possible to avoid them.

We had to face two men who might both believe that Autumn could have killed their mother, and my dear friend and I both knew that it wasn't going to be easy.

Chapter 17

AUTUMN PUT HER CELL phone on speaker so I could hear the conversation, but before she did, she said, "Suzanne, no matter what he says, you have to promise me that you won't say a word."

"What if he attacks you?" I asked her.

"Not even then. I mean it. If you can't make me that promise, then I can't let you listen in."

"Okay. I give you my word." It was going to be hard for me to keep quiet, but a promise was a promise.

I wasn't at all sure he was even going to pick up the phone, but after the seventh ring, just when I was certain that it was about to go to his voicemail, Jeff Marbury answered. "What." It amazed me how little emotion was conveyed in that one word. It was so cold, so completely sterile, that Autumn physically flinched from her estranged husband's response.

"We need to talk," she said tentatively.

"What is there to talk about?" he asked her. "My mother is dead."

"I know that, but as I told you before, I didn't kill her," she protested. "Jeff, I need to see you."

"Autumn, I'm sort of busy right now making funeral arrangements. I'm picking out her coffin."

"I'm sorry, but I have to see you. I wouldn't ask if it weren't important."

"Are you saying *this* isn't important?" he asked her icily.

"No, of course not. I just need five minutes of your time. I'll come to you, wherever you are." She glanced at me, and I did my best to smile reassuringly at her. It was brutal making her do this, but we really had no other choice.

"Meet me at the bench by the lake. You know the one. I'll be there in an hour."

"I'll be there," she said. "Jeff, I'm so sorry for your—"

He never heard the end of her statement, because he'd already hung up.

"There's no doubt about it, is there? He hates me," she said softly.

"Autumn, he's in shock right now. I'm sure that's not true."

"It's true, all right. I've lost him."

"I wasn't sure that you even still wanted him," I reminded her softly.

"We've been having some issues lately, but I've never stopped loving him. I realize that now. Suzanne, I've made a terrible mistake."

"Is it possible that you're in shock yourself?" I asked her gently. "After all, I know firsthand how tough it is to find a body like that."

"It's part of it, but it's not all of it. I suddenly can't bear the thought that my marriage is over."

She said it with such finality that my heart broke a little for her. "Don't write it off just yet. When we go see him at the lake, we'll get him to understand that you weren't involved."

"You don't get it. That bench was where I told him I was leaving him. He said that he never wanted to go back there again, that it made him feel dead inside. I'm guessing that he chose that spot to tell me that we are finished. I'm sorry, but you can't go with me."

"What? I have to," I protested.

"No. I need to do this alone," she said.

"Autumn, I can't even begin to understand what you must be going through, but it's not safe for you to meet him alone."

As soon as she realized what I was saying, she turned on me. "Do you think he's going to kill *me*? Jeff isn't some psychotic murderer, Suzanne. He loved me once, and I can't believe that there's not a part of him that still does."

I decided not to remind her that he had loved his mother, and there was a real possibility that he could have killed her. "We don't know that it's safe, though. I can't let you go there by yourself."

"There's nothing you can do to stop me. My mind is made up," she said.

"Can I at least be nearby watching, just in case?" I asked. "I should tell you that no matter what you say, I'm going to do that anyway. He won't see me, but I'll be able to witness anything that might happen. I'm sorry, I know you're not all that happy with me right now, but I have to do this."

Autumn wanted to protest, I could see it in her expression, but after a moment, she finally slumped a bit. "Fine, but he can't know that you are there."

"He won't," I said. "I've picked up a few things over the years. He won't see me."

"You'd better be right, or you and I are going to have a problem."

I didn't doubt it. "It's going to be okay."

"If only saying it made it so," she answered.

We were a full ten minutes early, but Jeff was already there ahead of us. "Give me two minutes before you join him," I said as she stopped the car.

"You'd better be right about being able to make yourself invisible," she said as I got out.

"I am," I said. I looped around out of his line of vision and moved to a spot near some trees where I could see him sitting on the bench in question, but he couldn't see me.

After a few moments, I watched as Autumn joined him. I was close enough to hear anything but a whisper from where I was, so it should be fine. I knew she hated the idea of me watching them, but I wasn't about to let my friend take a chance with her life.

"Jeff, I didn't kill her," Autumn started off saying.

He didn't even look in her direction as she sat on the bench beside him. Instead, he kept staring out at the calm water, as though he were a statue and not a man.

"So you say," he said coolly.

"How can you even *think* that I would hurt her?" she asked, the pain obvious in her voice.

He appeared to be unmoved by her question, or her anguish. "Autumn, you have to admit that you two have been fighting for months," he said. "Ever since Adam came back."

"What does that tell you?" she asked. "Your brother was the *cause* of that friction, and you know it. He's resented me from the day we met."

Jeff turned to look at her. I only wished that I could see his eyes, but from the body language alone, there was nothing warm or welcoming in his pose. "He said you'd say that."

"Say what?"

"That everything that's been happening lately has been his fault."

"Well, isn't it at least *possible* that it's true?" she asked him, nearly pleading with him now.

"Are you blaming *him* for killing Mother?" he asked. "He couldn't have. We've been together all day."

"Every minute of it?" she asked.

Jeff shifted a bit on the bench, and I could finally see his face. A troubled look crossed it for a moment. "I had to make a few phone calls, but I wasn't gone for more than half an hour," he said.

"So he *could* have done it," she said.

Jeff clearly couldn't believe her bold statement. "What possible reason could he have to want to see our mother dead?"

"Jeff, I heard them arguing about money myself," she admitted. "Your mother cut him off financially. Did you know that? Why do you think he came back home? He was broke. He had nowhere else to go."

"That's all a lie," Jeff said.

Suddenly they weren't alone anymore.

I saw someone from the parking lot start toward the bench.

It was Adam, and he looked as though he was going to kill Autumn the moment he reached her.

I had no choice.

I had to defend my friend, no matter what I'd promised her.

I cut Adam off before he could get to Autumn. "Where do you think you're going?"

"Get out of my way, donut girl," he said as he tried to push past me.

I might not have looked like it, but I had strong hands from kneading dough for all those years. I latched onto his biceps and stopped him in his tracks. "You need to leave them alone."

"Let go of me," he said as he jerked his arm away, though not without a great deal of effort. "She's not going to get away with spreading lies about me."

"The thing is that we both know that she's not lying," I said.

"How could you possibly know anything about that?" he asked angrily as he got closer to me than I liked. "Did you put her up to this?" Then Adam grabbed both my arms and pulled my face toward his. Apparently I wasn't the only one who was stronger than they looked.

"Let go of her," Autumn said suddenly from behind me.

"She shouldn't be here," Adam said, not easing his grip at all.

"Neither should you," she countered as she tried to help me break his grip.

"Adam, stop it," Jeff commanded. "Let her go this instant!"

Only then did his brother ease his grip on me. I had a hunch that I was going to bruise, there was no doubt about that, but I couldn't tell Jake about the confrontation, because I was afraid of what he might do to Adam.

"She's butting into our lives when she doesn't have any justification to," the older brother said sullenly.

Jeff got up into his brother's face, and I saw the fury he was experiencing at that moment toward his brother, something that surprised me. "She could have you arrested for assault, you idiot! Do we really need to deal with that too, on top of someone murdering our mother?"

"No, of course not," Adam said as he took a few steps backward. Whether he was genuinely sorry or not, I could not tell. "I'm sorry," he said without really looking into my eyes.

"Adam," Jeff scolded him, "you need to do better than that."

Where had this man suddenly come from, leaping to my defense against his own brother? Was he genuinely concerned for my feelings, or was he just trying to keep his brother out of trouble?

"I lost my mind for a second," Adam said as he finally made eye contact with me. "I'm under a great deal of stress right now. Please forgive me."

I was about to dismiss his apology and call the police anyway as I reached for my cell phone when I glanced over at Autumn. She was pleading with me with her gaze not to do anything, mouthing the words "Please don't," over and over again.

After that, I couldn't see how I could follow through. I put my cell phone away as I said, "I won't call the police." Adam looked a little too smug when I said it, so I added, "But if you ever lay one finger on me again, I'll call my husband."

"I understand," he said, trying to brush off what he thought was an idle threat.

"I don't think you do," I said. "So let me paint you a picture. He's a state police investigator who would punish you for touching me in anger in more ways than the legal system ever could." It wasn't an idle threat, either. Jake had a side to him that he presented to the world that was calm and law abiding, but when it came to someone hurting me, even a little, I'd hate to see what he was capable of. Frankly, it was another reason I didn't want to report the physical assault.

I was afraid of what he might do.

But I didn't want Adam to think that I was hiding behind my husband, either. I stepped in close and whispered just so he could hear me. "I'm not someone you want to mess with, either. Trust me, you don't want to find out what I'm capable of."

I took a step back and smiled at him. I think that was what threw him off the most. He clearly thought I was crazy, and I couldn't say for sure that he might not be right at that very moment.

Either way, I didn't think I'd have any more trouble with Adam Marbury.

"Let's get out of here," Jeff said as he roughly grabbed his brother's arm.

"We're not finished talking," Autumn told her estranged husband.

"There's really nothing more to say," Jeff answered.

"Ever?" she asked as tears began to creep down her cheeks.

Jeff clearly couldn't even bring himself to look at her. Maybe he was indeed finished with her once and for all.

Either way, the two men got into his car and drove away.

I turned to Autumn, who was still watching as they vanished. "I'm sorry I intervened. Adam looked as though he wanted to kill you, and I couldn't stand by and let that happen."

"And you ended up getting hurt instead," she said as she turned back to me. "Are you okay?"

"I'm fine," I said. My arms were still a bit sore, but if I was lucky, maybe I wouldn't bruise after all. I hated the thought of explaining those marks to Jake and where that conversation might lead.

"You were pretty cool under fire back there," Autumn said.

"How about you? You were the one who jumped to my defense. Thanks for doing that, by the way."

"Jeff argued that they didn't kill their mother," Autumn said in a broken voice. "I thought I could challenge him on it, but I couldn't bring myself to push him after he looked at me with those dead eyes."

"From what he said though, there was at least half an hour when they were apart," I said, recalling the conversation I'd overheard. "That would leave plenty of time for Adam to sneak back over to your old house and kill his mother without Jeff knowing about it."

"What you're not saying is that same scenario works for Jeff, too," Autumn said with a sigh. "How did things go so wrong so quickly?" she asked me.

I didn't have an answer for her. "We're doing the best we can," I said as I glanced at my watch. "Listen, we've got an hour before we have to meet Mr. Charleston. What do you think about going back to your place and grabbing a bite to eat?"

"I'd rather not have to face making anything right now," she admitted. "Do you have any interest in going back to the Blue Ridge Café for dinner?"

"I'm all for it, if you can stand being around people after what just happened," I said. "If Cheswick is anything like home, half the town has already convicted you of homicide. I hate to be so blunt, but you need to face that fact right now."

"Let them talk," Autumn said wearily. "It won't be the first time I was the subject of gossip around here."

"For moving out, sure, but not for murder," I corrected her. "Believe me, it can get pretty ugly. I've been accused of the same thing a few times in the past myself, and it can really get you down."

"You believe me, though, and that's all I need," she said as she tried to smile, despite what had just happened. "Come on. It's my treat."

"How could I possibly pass that up?" I asked her as we headed back for her car. I knew life was about to get even harder for my friend, but she was right about one thing. She had me in her corner, and I wasn't about to desert her in her time of need. Anybody can be a friend when everything is sunshine and daisies. A true friend is one who stands right beside you when everyone else is doing their very best to bring you down. It was almost, and I meant not at all really, worth being attacked just to see who you could actually count on in times of trouble.

No matter what, I was going to stand by my friend, even if it meant putting my own name, and my life, in the path of peril.

Otherwise, what good did friendship really do anyone?

Chapter 18

"YOU'RE BACK," DAVIS said with glee as we walked into the restaurant again. His was the only smile we got. People at the nearby tables averted their gazes as soon as they realized that Autumn was among them. Small towns in the South were the same everywhere; gossip happened at lightning speed, whether it was rooted in the truth or not. "Welcome, ladies."

"Thanks," Autumn said as we took a seat near the back. A family was sitting at the table beside us, and as soon as we sat down, the father threw a twenty-dollar bill on the table and ushered his wife and two kids out of the café. Another couple sitting nearby left before ordering, but only after they took a moment to glare at us as though we'd ruined their days.

"I'm sorry about that," Autumn said as she started to stand. "We're not doing your business much good by eating here."

"Sit back down," Davis said firmly. In a voice much louder than it needed to be, he said, "Autumn, we've been friends for the past several months, and I'm not going to let a little idle gossip change that. Anyone who doesn't like it is free to eat somewhere else."

"Really, I don't mind," Autumn continued, still clearly unsure about how she felt about being under such scrutiny.

"Well, I do," Davis said as he left his table and sat down across from me. "You're not going to just stand there, are you?"

"No, sir," she said with a smile as she took her place again. "Thanks, Davis."

"There's no need to thank me," he said. "I know you didn't kill Cecile Marbury."

"You might be the *only* one in town who thinks that, including my husband," Autumn said as she tried to slump down in her seat a little.

"Jeff's had a great shock," Davis said. "Give him some time. He'll come around."

"Not unless we find who really killed Mrs. Marbury," I said.

He turned to me. "You're the donutmaking sleuth, am I right?"

"How could you possibly know that?" I asked him.

"The police chief's been coming here for breakfast since she was in high school," he said softly. "We talk, and I've got to tell you, she's worried about you."

"Outshining her?" Autumn asked.

Davis looked a little reluctant to share the truth, but I had a hunch about what he was hinting at. "She doesn't want me mucking up her case," I said.

Davis nodded. "True enough, but once she left, I did a little digging online myself. You've got quite the track record when it comes to murder, young lady."

"Thank you?" I asked, more of a question than a statement.

"I think it's marvelous what you've done in the past. What do you say? Can you help our girl here out?" he asked as he gestured toward Autumn.

"I'm trying," I said. "The truth is that it's tough getting anyone to come clean with us."

Davis nodded. "I get that." Lowering his voice, he asked, "Where do things stand so far? Don't worry, you can trust me."

Could I though, could I really? I didn't know this man well at all, and besides, he'd just shared information with us that he'd gotten from the chief of police. Why should I think that wouldn't be a two-way street? I'd nearly made up my mind to gently refuse his request when Autumn surprised me by speaking up first. "We're looking at Jeff, Adam, Annie, Mr. Charleston, and even Lee, though that's ridiculous, if you ask me."

Davis seemed to take it all in before he spoke. "I'm not so sure. He's got it bad for you, Autumn. I could see him fighting with Cecile about you, and he's got a temper."

That seemed to surprise her. "Really? I haven't seen any sign of it."

"That's because he's gotten good at keeping it out of plain sight," Davis said. "When he was in high school, another kid made fun of his girlfriend. Lee punched him in the nose and broke it with one hit. I wish that I could say that was the only time something like that happened, but if I did, I'd be lying."

"Still, that was in high school," Autumn said a little nervously.

"Which was quite a bit more recent than it was for the rest of us," Davis added.

Herbert chose that time to come out of the kitchen, and when he spotted us, he frowned. Oh, no. Were we about to be on the other end of his wrath?

"I want to talk to you about what happened," he said as he stood over Autumn. Before either one of us could say a word, he quickly added, "There's no way you could have done what some people are saying that you did. I don't believe it, and neither does anyone else with the least amount of sense."

"Thanks for that," Autumn said, clearly relieved by his declaration.

"Are you two having the special?" he asked.

"I don't even need to know what it is, but I want it," I said as I nodded. "If you made it, that's good enough for me."

"Make it two," Autumn said.

"See?" Herbert asked as he broke out into a grin. "I told you these two ladies were our kind of people, Davis."

"I never denied it, did I?" the older man asked. "Now go fetch their food."

Herbert grinned upon receiving the order. "I let him tell me what to do. It makes him feel good to act like he's the one in charge around here."

After the cook disappeared back into the kitchen, I asked Davis, "Does he always act like that?"

"The truth is that I wouldn't want to run this café without him, so I give him a lot of latitude. What does it hurt? It makes him happy, and when he's happy, his cooking is at its best. You're in for a real treat this evening. He made a meatloaf that's so tender and juicy it will break your heart, the mashed potatoes are from the farmer's market, and the green beans, too. He sautés the beans in olive oil and some spice blend that he won't tell me about, and it's all amazing. I hope you like sweet tea, because unless you ask for something else, that's what you're going to get."

Ten seconds later a lovely dark-haired girl around eighteen, with Maria embroidered on her short apron, came over to the table with two teas. "Do you need anything while I'm here, boss?" she asked Davis after she delivered our drinks.

"I'm fine, darlin'. How did finals go?"

"I aced them all, Grandpa," she said with a smile as she kissed his cheek.

"No surprise there," he said. "You always were the smartest one in the family."

"Besides you, you mean," she said with a broad grin.

"I thought that went without saying," he said, smiling just the same.

After she was gone, Davis said, "That young lady is heading off to Harvard in the fall."

"Wow, that's got to be expensive," I said, the words blurting out before I could filter them.

"It would be, but she's getting a full ride. I think that's what she called it. It means they're paying for everything. Can you imagine that?"

"She must really be bright," Autumn said.

Davis leaned forward. "I'd never admit it in front of her, but I suspect that she actually might even *be* smarter than me." His grin was infectious, and our moods began to lighten. It had been a tough day, especially since Autumn had found her mother-in-law's body, but Davis was doing his best to ease our mood.

When the food came, it looked as amazing as I'd expected. Instead of getting a meal like ours, Maria brought her grandfather a slice of peach cobbler with vanilla bean ice cream on top. "Don't tell Momma I gave you this," she whispered as she offered the older man a wink and a smile.

"The things I haven't told your mother over the years would fill an ocean," Davis said as he started to dig in with relish.

I took my first bite of meatloaf and couldn't help but smile as well. It was truly incredible, from the meat itself to the tomato-based topping that covered it. The potatoes were firm and yet still creamy, and the green beans were good enough to eat as a main course all on their own. I saw Herbert peek out from the kitchen to see what we thought, and I stood up and started applauding. Autumn soon joined me, and we gave him a two-person standing ovation. He actually blushed from the attention, dismissed us with a wave of his hand, and then went back to work. I could see his grin as he ducked back, and Davis shook his head. "He's going to be impossible for the next few days."

"It really is amazing," I said as I sat and took up my fork again.

"I know. I keep worrying that he's going to realize that his skills are being underutilized here, but so far, he seems to be happy enough running my little kitchen."

"Why would he ever leave?" Autumn asked as she touched the older man's arm. "You're a wonderful boss."

"I do my best," Davis said. After he finished his treat, but well before we made it through our meals, he jotted down what looked like a bill and slid it across the table to me.

"It's my treat this evening," Autumn said as she reached for it.

He just smiled and walked up front and out of the restaurant after leaving behind the customary five for his granddaughter. Autumn looked at the total, and then she frowned.

"Listen, if it's too much, I can cover it for you," I said. I had no idea what her money situation was at the moment, but it couldn't have been easy living on her own without a job.

"That's not it," she said as she shoved the check toward me. In precise handwriting, it said,

"Dinner's on the house. Meet me in the park when you're finished. We need to talk."

"What do you suppose that was all about?" Autumn asked me as I folded the note up and put it in my pocket.

"He must have something to say," I told her as I looked around the café. Several folks had been watching the three of us for the entire meal, and there was no doubt in my mind that they'd been hanging on every word that we'd said. "Let's do as he asked."

"Fine, but I'm still leaving a tip," she said as she dug into her wallet and pulled out a ten-dollar bill.

"That's too much," Maria said with a frown when she spotted it a minute later.

"For that meal? I'm not at all sure that it's enough."

"Tell you what. I'll split it with you," she said as she took the five her grandfather had left her and handed it to Autumn. "I shouldn't even take that, but my scholarship doesn't cover everything, and I hear Boston is expensive."

"Congratulations on Harvard, by the way," I said.

"Thanks. I almost turned it down, but Grandpa talked me into it."

"Why on earth would you pass up an opportunity like that?" Autumn asked her.

The young woman looked around the café wistfully. "This is the only home I've ever known. It's going to be tough leaving it, and him," she said. "I don't know how many years he's got left, and I don't want to miss any of them."

"If I know your grandfather, I'm guessing that there's no way he'd ever let you stay here when you've got something like that available to you," I said.

"I'd say you know him pretty well. I've taught him how to text, and next we're going to work on Facetime so we can see each other when we chat. He's picking it all up pretty fast." She waved the ten in the air as she added, "Thanks for this. Dinner's on the house."

"So we heard. Thanks, Maria," Autumn said.

"Come back anytime," she said, and then she lowered her head toward us as she added, "For what it's worth, I'm on your side, too."

It was nice to know that Davis, Herbert, and Maria had our backs, even if most of the rest of the residents didn't.

After all, any port in the storm was a good port.

I couldn't wait to hear what Davis had to say. It had to be juicy, or he never would have insisted that we meet him in the park.

If we got lucky, it might just help lead us exactly where we wanted to go. I was well aware that we were under a time crunch that I'd rarely faced before. The chief of police could decide to arrest Autumn at any moment, and it felt as though we had hours, not days, to figure out who had killed Cecile Marbury.

I just hoped that we were up for the challenge.

Chapter 19

"SORRY ABOUT THE CLOAK-and-dagger stuff, but I needed to talk to you two where no one else could hear us." Davis looked around the park, and naturally, so did we. No one was paying any attention to us, which was a nice change of pace after being under so much scrutiny in the café.

"We understand," Autumn said. "It's kind of brave of you to be willing to be seen with me at all."

"It's not brave at all," Davis said, dismissing her words casually. "You didn't do it, but I might have an idea about who might. Have you heard of a man named Henry Charleston?"

"As a matter of fact, we're meeting with him in half an hour," I said as I glanced at my watch.

Davis nodded in approval. "I'm impressed. Did you know that Henry is under suspicion for syphoning off some of his clients' money?"

"No, that we hadn't heard," I said. "Do you know anything specific?"

"Nothing concrete you can use, if that's what you're asking," Davis said. "I just happened to overhear two of my wealthier customers whispering about Henry one day last week. Word was that a certain older woman with a great deal of money caught him doing it. She gave him one week to repay every penny, or she was going to the police."

"Were they talking about Cecile?" Autumn asked.

"That I can't say," Davis admitted, "but it figures that it very well might be."

"Who's your source?" I asked him. "Maybe we can get one of the ladies to speak with us."

"Sorry, but I can't do that," Davis said. "No offense."

"None taken," I said. "I respect that. Even if it wasn't Cecile, we can still use it against Charleston."

"Shouldn't we tell Chief Seaborne?" Autumn asked us.

"What exactly would you tell her?" Davis asked. "This is thirdhand knowledge at best. No, I thought about mentioning it to Sam myself, but I thought you might be able to use it to your advantage first."

"I appreciate your faith in us," I said.

"Hey, I figure Autumn at least deserves twenty-four hours to dig into this before the world comes crashing down on her," Davis said.

"Do you have anything else we might be able to use?" I asked him.

"Annie Greenway," he said.

"What about her?" I asked.

"She and Cecile had a fight not twenty feet from here three days ago," Davis said. "I was pretending to take a nap on that bench over there, so it was easy to eavesdrop." Before we could comment on that, he grinned. "Hey, I'm a harmless old man. I get my kicks where I can."

"I doubt you've ever been harmless a day in your life," I told him with a grin.

"I knew I liked you for a reason," he said.

"What was the argument about?" Autumn asked him.

"You," he said.

"Me? Why would they fight about me?"

"Annie wanted Cecile to put pressure on Jeff to dump you, but she wouldn't do it. Annie was furious and said something snippy to Cecile, which was the wrong thing to do." He patted Autumn's hand. "You should feel good that the old gal defended you," he said. "I know things have been strained between you lately, but she honestly did care for you, Autumn."

My former roommate teared up suddenly, and I offered her a hankie. "Are you okay?"

"As a matter of fact, it's the nicest thing I've heard in a while," she said. "How did Annie react to that?"

"She was livid," Davis said. "I believe a bit of the woman's true self slipped out. She said that they weren't finished discussing it. When Cecile said she most decidedly was, Annie stared at her for ten full seconds before she said, 'That's what you think.' Cecile honestly looked a bit frightened when Annie stormed off. I felt chills myself, and her vitriol hadn't even been directed at me. I was about to abandon my ruse and offer Cecile some comfort when she shook her head slightly and then hurried off. I'll tell you, Annie Greenway is a powder keg waiting to blow. If I were the two of you, I'd be careful around that gal, and don't turn your back on her."

"Good to know," I said. "What do you know about Adam Marbury?"

"I didn't like him when he was a kid, and I haven't seen any reason to change my opinion since he's gotten back into town. He's the kind of guy who will pat you on the back with one hand while he's stealing your wallet with the other."

"He sounds like a real prize," I said.

"Jeff is the only one in the entire lot I'd give you two cents for," Davis said. "He's a good man, deep down, Autumn."

"Would a good man turn his back on me?" she asked him, tearing up again.

"Pardon me for saying so, but aren't *you* the one who moved out?" Davis asked, his voice gentle and calm.

"If I stayed in that house one more day, I would have been the one lying on the floor, not Cecile!" she snapped. "I *had* to get away."

Davis clouded up. "Did he raise a hand to you, child?"

"Jeff? No, of course not," she said, apparently caught off guard by the mere thought of it. "Something was going on there, though. I didn't feel safe, so I couldn't stay."

Davis nodded. "I wondered why you moved out so suddenly. I'll tell you one thing, Lee Graham was happy enough to hear it. That boy's got it bad for you, Autumn. You haven't done anything to encourage that, have you?"

"No, of course not!" Autumn practically shouted her words, and I wondered if she wasn't protesting a bit too much.

"Easy," Davis said, holding up his gnarled old hands. "I meant nothing by it. I'm just saying, he's clearly got the itch when it comes to you."

"Well, I never encouraged it, not for one second," Autumn said.

Somehow we'd gotten off topic. "Davis, is there anything else you can tell us that might help us?"

He shook his head. "No, that's all I've got. I'll keep my ear to the ground, but I'm afraid you're both on your own."

"You've helped more than we can say," I told him. Almost as an afterthought, I leaned over and kissed him lightly on the cheek. "Thank you."

"You're welcome," he said with a smile. "I've got to tell you, I wasn't expecting such a generous reward. Here I thought I was just doing a good deed, and I get a kiss for my troubles."

"Two, actually," Autumn said as she kissed his other cheek. As she pulled back, she looked around and saw that three or four people had seen her gesture. "I'm so sorry. I didn't mean to drag you into this by kissing your cheek."

"Young lady, the day I refuse to help a damsel in distress, or turn down a kiss on the cheek from one, is one day past when I want to keep on living."

I had to laugh. "Your wife was a lucky woman, Davis," I said.

He grinned at me. "I was the lucky one. Would you like to see a picture of her?"

We were going to be late if we didn't leave for our meeting immediately, but I didn't care. Not only did I not want to spurn the dear man's invitation, but I was honestly curious about her. "I'd love to."

He dug out his wallet and handed me a faded sepia picture of a young woman in her late teens sporting short dark curls and Mary Jane shoes. She was ordinary enough in the looks department, except for her smile. It lit up her entire face, and I could see the warmth and goodness coming through the photograph. "She was a real beauty," I said as I handed it back to him.

"She was pretty enough, but when she smiled, the whole world around her became a brighter place."

"You must miss her terribly," Autumn said.

"In a way, but in another very real way, I carry her with me wherever I go," he said as he tapped his heart. "Now I'd better get back before Herbert and Maria run the place into the ground without me," he said with a wink.

"Thanks again," I called out to him as we all stood.

"The pleasure was all mine, especially the reward," he said as he doffed a hat he wasn't even wearing.

We both watched him walk back to the café with a spring in his step. After he was back inside, I turned to Autumn. "Are you ready to brace Henry Charleston?"

"I'm ready if you are," she said.

"Then let's go. We don't even have to drive. His office is two blocks from here, and by the time we get there, we'll be right on schedule for our appointment."

"Wouldn't you rather drive?" Autumn asked me.

"No, this will give me a bit of time to get ready for him. I'm guessing he's going to be a pretty smooth talker, and I have to be at my best if I'm going to get him to tell us the truth."

"Why do you think he's so slick?" she asked me as we started off.

"He talked Cecile Marbury into letting him handle her money, and we both know that your late mother-in-law was not an easy woman to convince of anything."

"You can say that again," Autumn said.

We spent the rest of the walk in near silence as I prepared myself for the verbal battle to come. I was going to try to outwit a man who made his living being fast on his feet, but I had one thing going for me that he didn't realize.

I knew about his troubled business relationship with Cecile Marbury.

Even if she wasn't the mystery woman in the conversation that Davis had overheard, it figured that if Charleston played fast and loose with one client's money, it wasn't that big a stretch to imagine he did it with them all.

Henry Charleston's office was elegant, from the expensive artwork adorning the walls to the antique furniture everywhere to the Oriental rug on the hardwood floor. Charleston matched his décor, his three-piece suit cut to perfection, his silver hair perfectly styled, and his wingtip shoes polished to a blinding gleam. He was starting to get portly, but his tailor had done a good job disguising it, at least so far. He looked startled to see my attire, blue jeans and a T-shirt, but he was even more surprised to see Autumn Marbury with me. "Mrs. Marbury, I didn't realize you were coming. So sorry for your loss," he said automatically.

"Thank you," she said. "I'm the one who recommended you to Suzanne. After all, you seem to have done so well with my late mother-in-law's funds." There was a twist of disdain in the last few words, and I was afraid that she'd overplayed it when she spoke again. "However, after learning of a few things since, I'm afraid I won't be able to recommend you after all."

What was she doing? Grace had gone rogue before in our investigations, and I'd even come to expect it, but I hadn't seen this coming, at least not from Autumn. Still, I had to play along. "There are some troubling rumors that are starting to come to light, sir," I said as I frowned.

"Please, sit. I'll do whatever it takes to assure you that I've done *nothing* to deserve any negative things you might be hearing about me." He was backpedaling as fast as he could to keep us in his office, and I had to wonder if he'd managed to dig into my mother's assets in the short time since I'd made the appointment. I made it a point not to ask Momma what she was worth, but I had a hunch that even my wildest guess wouldn't even be close to the true amount.

"You and Mrs. Marbury were arguing about money," I said. It was a statement, not a question, and I waited for him to deny it.

"That's true enough," he said.

Did he actually just admit it? No way did I ever get that lucky when I was questioning a suspect. "Go on," I said.

"Against my advice, she had me move some of her funds into an account that I didn't approve of, but she claimed that it was her money and her decision, so what could I do? Unfortunately, it turned out badly rather quickly. She blamed me for not objecting harder. It wasn't all that great a shock to me. When clients go against my advice and lose money, they often blame me for their bad decisions. I don't have power of attorney. I can't make them do *anything*; my position is to advise."

"What was the investment?" I asked. After all, if he was using a fake entity as an excuse in order to steal from her, he would be reluctant to give out that kind of information.

"I'd rather not say," he said. "I consider it privileged between my clients and myself."

"You're not a doctor or a lawyer, so nothing is *really* privileged information, at least not legally."

"But you're not an attorney yourself," he said. "In fact, you're a donutmaker." He said it as though it were an insult.

"Yes, that's true enough, but I'm about to become a very rich donutmaker."

He nodded. "I'm not sure what else I can tell you, but if you'll trust me to guide you through difficult financial waters, I assure you that I'll keep you afloat, no matter how troubling the shoals ahead of you might be." It was clearly a canned speech, but I had to give him credit. He said it with a great deal of conviction and panache.

"When did you last see my mother-in-law?" Autumn asked him.

He looked surprised by her interjection. "This morning, as a matter of fact," Charleston admitted. "She summoned me to your former home." He shivered for a moment before adding, "It's difficult to believe that two hours later, she was gone."

"She didn't vanish, Mr. Charleston," I said icily. "She was murdered."

"Of course. I can assure you though, the dear lady was very much alive when I left."

"Is there any way you can prove that?" Autumn asked.

"How does one go about proving a negative?" he asked her. "I appreciate what you've been going through today, but I'm not sure it's proper for you to be present during this meeting."

We'd gotten everything we were going to get from this man, so I decided to shoot one last salvo. "I have one last question for you. Will your books stand up under an audit, sir?"

Charleston feigned surprise at my comment. "They have in the past, and I'm sure they will again. Once a year, I undergo one voluntarily, and my records have been deemed immaculate every single time."

"I'm not talking about something general," I pushed. "I'm talking about Cecile Marbury's account specifically. You have to know that the Marbury brothers are not going to just take your word for the state of their mother's financial affairs."

Was it my imagination, or did he flinch a bit from that last statement? "When and if they ever decide to review her investments, I'll be more than happy to explain everything to them."

Autumn shrugged. "I imagine they're going to hire an outside auditor to go over the accounts for them," she said. "In fact, as soon as we leave here, I'm going to suggest they do just that, the sooner the better."

He was definitely paler now. "I was under the impression that you and your husband were estranged."

"We might be, but we still talk every day, and I know that he takes my opinion seriously. Is there anything else you want to add before we leave?"

He shook his head. "I'm afraid my time is up." As he stood, he offered to shake both our hands, and when he took mine, I found that it was cold and clammy. "Ms. Hart, I look forward to hearing from you soon."

He couldn't get us out of there fast enough, though.

Once we were outside, I started to say something when Autumn held up one hand and pulled out her cell phone. "It's me. No, I don't want to talk about that. Just listen. Cecile's money was being controlled by Henry Charleston. You knew that? Well, did you know that at least one older woman has accused him of embezzling from her? I don't know if he took anything from your mother, but if I were you, I'd get a forensic accountant on his books tomorrow at the latest, tonight if you can manage it. I just left him, and he looked as though he'd seen a ghost when I brought up your mother's name. That's not important. You need to do something, Jefferson. Good-bye." After she put her phone away and we started walking back to the car, she said, "Well, at least I tried to warn him."

"Did he want to know what you were doing there in the first place?" I asked.

"He did, but I wasn't about to tell him what we're doing."

"Will he follow your advice?" I asked her.

"If it were just him, maybe not, but I'm willing to bet that Adam is going to jump all over this. Unless I miss my guess, he'll have a court order, and someone will be digging into those books by midnight tonight."

"How can you be so sure?" I asked her as we approached her car.

"It's been my experience in the past that a liar expects you to lie to him, and a cheater does the same. Adam will follow through. I guarantee it. So, what happens now?"

I was about to answer when I spotted someone leaning against Autumn's car.

Apparently Chief Samantha Seaborne wasn't quite done with us for the day yet.

Chapter 20

"YOU TWO HAVE BEEN BUSY little bees, haven't you?" the chief asked us as we approached her.

"There are a lot of people who want to express their grief over us all losing Cecile," Autumn said seamlessly.

"I bet," she said. "Is that really your story, that you've been making the rounds giving folks a chance to tell you how sorry they are about your mother-in-law?"

"Late mother-in-law," I corrected her. "Have you found out who did it yet?"

Chief Seaborne looked at me a moment before she spoke. The icy stare may have worked on some people, but I was immune to it, and not just because I was married to a former state police investigator. I'd had better training than that. I'd had my mother give me the exact same stare the entire time I'd been growing up, and if she hadn't been able to crack me, Chief Seaborne didn't stand a chance. "The famous donut detective," she said with a bit of a smirk.

"I make donuts for a living. I only step in to help solve homicides when the police don't have any luck doing it themselves."

"Really? Is that the tone you're going to take with me?"

I wasn't about to back down. She was trying to bully me, and I didn't take well to that, not ever. "I'm just matching your general demeanor," I said calmly. "If you want to have a discussion, I'm ready to talk anytime, but if you're trying to intimidate me into dropping this, then I'm afraid that you're wasting your time."

The police chief took that in for a few moments, and then she turned to Autumn. "Is that your opinion, too?"

"We just want to know who killed Cecile," Autumn said flatly. "We don't mean any offense to you, Chief."

"I beg to differ. You're saying you don't think I can solve this murder, so you're going to step in and do it for me," she said.

"We never said that," I corrected her.

"Maybe not in so many words, but your actions speak louder than your words. You both need to knock it off, and I mean now."

"Or else?" I asked her.

She looked at me quizzically. "Or else?"

"Usually there's a threat attached when someone says that," I told her.

"I don't threaten. I deliver on my promises."

"Then promise us you'll find Cecile's killer," Autumn said. "There are plenty of suspects besides me, you know."

"I know you think you're helping, but in actuality, you're not," she said.

"We're trying to clear Autumn's name," I answered. "That's all we're trying to do."

"If she didn't do it, then she's got nothing to fear from me, but that's an awfully big if."

"And that's why we're digging into it ourselves," I said, getting frustrated with this woman's attempt at scaring us off the case. "It's funny, but my husband spoke highly of you when I mentioned your name to him."

"Doesn't that count for anything with you?" she asked me.

"The truth of the matter is that I haven't seen anything yet to justify his opinion of you," I admitted. I'd gone too far, and I knew it as soon as I said it. "I'm sorry I said that last bit, I truly am, but we can't quit."

"You should know that the *only* thing you're accomplishing is making Autumn look even guiltier than she does now," the chief said. "There are quite a few prominent people in the community who are howling for me to lock her up even as we speak."

"Based on circumstantial evidence that doesn't hold up to scrutiny?" I asked.

"Who exactly are you trying to convince of that? She had the means, the motive, *and* the opportunity. You should know by now that it could all hang her, except for my reluctance to put the cuffs on her right now."

"If you do, we both know that her lawyer will have her out in time for bed," I said, hoping that it was true. I wasn't sure how good an attorney Tom had become, but he was all that we had at the moment.

"Maybe, maybe not," she said. After a moment, the chief shrugged. "Okay, I admit it. I underestimated you," she said as she smiled softly at me.

"What do you mean?"

"I thought I could scare you off, but obviously you're not going to give this up. I could arrest you both for obstruction of justice, but at least so far you haven't done anything I can hang you with. So far."

"You'd be amazed by how we might be able to help if you'd just give us a chance," I told her.

"Thanks, but no thanks. I'm doing just fine without you both, but you'd better be careful."

"Are you suddenly back to threatening us?" I asked her.

"No, but somebody out there is a killer, and if it isn't you, Mrs. Marbury, then it's someone who's not afraid of getting their hands dirty, if you follow me."

Autumn looked a bit disturbed by the statement, with good reason. I'd come close to dying on more than one occasion in the past because of an investigation, but I didn't see how we could just drop it and pretend as though nothing had happened, or that she hadn't already been tried and convicted by the gossip circulating around town. "We'll be careful," I said.

"I hope so, for both your sakes," she said as she walked away from us, heading back to her squad car, which was parked twenty feet away.

Autumn looked at me steadily before moving to get into her car. "Suzanne, are you sure this is still a good idea?"

"Do you want to live with the stigma of Cecile's death hanging over your head for the rest of your life? I can tell you that's what's going to happen if we don't crack this case, and fast."

"I know you're right," she said as she got into the car. "What do we do now?"

"Now we go back to your place and regroup," I said as I slid onto the seat on the other side.

"Really? It's still early," she answered.

"Not for me. Remember, I'm still on Daylight Donut Time," I replied with a grin.

"I keep forgetting," she said as we headed back to her cottage.

"It's easy enough to do," I said.

When we pulled into her long drive, I could swear that I saw someone running into the trees.

Apparently we had startled someone in the act of doing something I was pretty sure we weren't going to like.

"Stop the car!"

Autumn did as I asked, but she was clearly concerned about my sudden request. "Suzanne, what's going on?"

"I saw someone lurking in the trees," I said as I piled out of the car and headed to where I'd last seen the intruder. I couldn't even swear if it was a man or a woman because the glimpse had been so fleeting, but I knew that I'd seen someone.

"We don't have any weapons on us," Autumn shouted just behind me. Great. Let's announce to the world that we're unarmed.

"I've got a gun," I shouted, as much to Autumn as to whoever was ahead of us.

"What?" she screamed.

"Stop or I'll shoot," I commanded, even though I couldn't see anyone ahead of us. All I heard was rapidly fading noises through the underbrush, and I knew that we weren't going to be able to catch whoever had been there.

I stopped and leaned against a tree to catch my breath.

Autumn stopped just beside me. "Do you really have a gun?" she asked.

"No," I whispered, "but let's not advertise the fact, okay?"

"Okay," she said, clearly looking relieved.

"Does that mean that you don't?" I asked.

"You know how I feel about those things," I said.

"Fine. Do you have a softball bat or a golf club, by any chance?"

"Sorry, but you know me. I'm not very athletic," she confessed.

"I'm not asking you to play a round of golf with me or hit some fly balls, I'm talking about protection."

"You've already discovered that I have some cast iron pans in the kitchen," she said. "I've also got some pepper spray in my purse, if that helps."

"We might just end up needing both of them before this is all over," I replied.

"Who do you think it might have been?"

"I honestly don't know," I answered truthfully.

She paused a moment. "Do you think it might have been the killer?"

"It's a distinct possibility. We've been asking a great many questions around town. Any one of our suspects could be trying to get rid of us."

"You seem pretty nonchalant about it," Autumn said as we neared the cottage.

"It's not the first time it's happened to me," I admitted. "Besides, it just tells me that we struck a nerve with someone today."

"Any idea who?" she asked.

"No."

"Then what good does it do us?" The woman looked as though she was ready to start crying at the prospect of being stalked by a killer, which, when I thought about it, was a pretty reasonable reaction to that particular situation. Had I been digging into murder too long if the fact that we'd scared someone made me happy?

"We push harder," I said. "How do you deal with a bully? You walk up and punch him in the nose. It's the only language they understand."

She stopped and frowned at me, and then a few tears started to track down her cheeks. "This is getting out of hand. Maybe we should just quit and let the police handle this."

"Is that what you really want, to live the rest of your life with this hanging over your head? What if they never find the killer? There will be nowhere for you to turn. You need to put on your big-girl pants and help me figure out what really happened to Cecile."

Autumn managed to stop crying before it broke out in full force, and after a moment, she looked at me curiously and asked, "Have you really punched someone in the nose?"

"As a matter of fact, in sixth grade I hit Billy Klingman for pushing Harry Vicker down in the playground, but I was speaking metaphorically."

"You've really changed since college, haven't you?" she asked me.

"What do you mean? I hope I have. Haven't we all?"

"I just mean that the old Suzanne would never go looking for trouble, at least not like this," she said softly.

"Well, the old Suzanne hadn't seen the things that the current one has. I won't apologize for trying to keep you from being charged with murder. If that means that I have to ruffle a few feathers in the process, then so be it."

Autumn took a step back. "Hey, take it easy. I wasn't criticizing you."

"Really? It sure sounded that way to me." I was on edge because of the investigation, but there was more to it than that. Being with Autumn again made me revert to a more combative stage in my life where if I saw someone doing something out of character, I wouldn't hesitate to call them on it. Age, and maybe a little wisdom, had taught me to

be a little more judicious with my criticisms, but apparently being with
Autumn again was bringing some of the old black-and-white Suzanne
back, instead of the woman who saw a great many shades of gray. It
made me act a little harsher with her than I should have, but I couldn't
seem to help myself.

"I wasn't, honestly. It's just that sometimes you act exactly like the
girl I remember, and other times you're someone completely different."

"I don't deny it," I said. After a long pause, I added, "You know, I'm
not the only one who's changed."

"Are you talking about me?" Autumn asked, a hint of pain in her
question.

"Let's not go there," I said as I started back. "We have enough trouble on our hands without adding anything to it."

She put a hand on my shoulder. "No, I want to know."

"Okay, if you're sure," I said after taking a deep breath. "What happened to you? The old Autumn would never do anything halfway like
moving out but *not* divorcing her husband. You clearly care for the
man, and I know some bad things have been happening to you and
around you lately, but when did you get so timid?" They were hard
words, but they'd needed to be said. Something had to snap her out
of her fearfulness, and if I could shake her up, I would. Replacing the
sting in my voice with gentleness, I added, "I know it's been rough on
you, but this is not the time to falter or second-guess what we're doing.
We've got a killer worried about us, so we need to push all of our suspects harder, no matter what the consequences might be."

"Even if it ruins what little chance I have to be happy?" she asked
me.

"If it's meant to be, you have to believe that it will all work out in
the end," I answered.

"What would you do if you were in my shoes?"

"Exactly what we're doing," I said as I started walking again. We were at the side of the cottage now where the bedroom windows were when something in the brush caught my eye.

When I stopped suddenly, Autumn asked, "Is something wrong?"

I knelt down and pulled away some of the pine needles that had been carefully piled up around the object that had caught my eye.

It was a small wireless speaker from the look of it.

Apparently the voices I'd heard the night before had been real enough.

It looked as though someone was trying to convince both of us that we were going crazy.

Chapter 21

AUTUMN STARTED TO SAY something when I put my fingers on her lips gently. After motioning her away from the electronic device, I waited until I was pretty sure we were far enough away that if there *was* a microphone attached, it wouldn't be able to pick up our conversation. Still, it might pay us to whisper, so I said softly, "You can talk now, but softly."

"Why would anyone do this?" she whispered.

"It's pretty obvious, isn't it? They want you to think that you're losing your mind," I answered in kind. "They made a mistake, though. They tried to get to me, too, and I'm not in nearly the fragile state you're in."

"I'm not fragile," she said harshly. "I'm just as tough as you remember."

It was good to see the fire back in her. Maybe my scolding had acted as a wake-up call for her. After all, she was in the fight of her life, and she needed every ounce of that old spirit she could resurrect. "It's good to have you back," I said with a grin.

"You know what? It's good to be back. Should we get that thing and smash it into a million pieces?"

"As tempting as that sounds, I've got a different idea."

"I'm listening," she said.

"Okay, here's what we do. We go back inside and pretend that we never found that thing in the first place. In an hour when it's dark, we pretend to go to bed, but then we sneak out the back and see who comes to retrieve it."

"What makes you think they'll come back for it?" she asked me.

"They did last night. I'm positive that I searched that spot this morning, and it wasn't there. We might not have seen it tonight, but

I think we startled whoever left it before they could hide it properly. That's going to be their downfall."

"We need a weapon, then," she said. "I might be able to find something better than a frying pan."

"Don't discount the value of one of those," I said.

"Don't forget that I have pepper spray, too. Would that help?"

"It couldn't hurt," I admitted. "Okay, are you ready to start acting normal?"

"It's probably going to be a stretch, but if you can do it, I'm pretty sure that I can, too." She was grinning as she said it, and I was happy that there was no residual anger left over from our earlier spat. We'd been that way in college too, being able to argue one second and be best friends again the next. I valued that quality in her, and now that I had the spirited woman I knew back with me, I started feeling better about the odds of us finding the killer and somehow managing to get out of this alive.

"How about a snack?" she asked me as we returned to the cottage.

"Sounds good," I said. After grabbing one of Autumn's heavier cast iron pans, I conducted a quick search of the place, the pan ready to strike at the slightest provocation. I hadn't really been expecting anyone to be lurking in a closet or under a bed, but I knew that we'd both feel better if we were sure that we were alone.

"Are we good?" Autumn asked as I rejoined her in the kitchen. She was making a pan of triple chocolate brownies, our favorite treat when we'd roomed together so many years before.

"We're all set," I said. "How long before the goodies come out?"

"We have another sixteen minutes," she said.

"Perfect. I have just enough time to call Jake."

"Give him my love," she said as she started cleaning up the kitchen.

"You bet," I answered with a grin.

"Hey, sweetie. How was your day?" I asked when he picked up.

"The truth is, you were right."

"Not that I don't love hearing it, but about what exactly?"

"I pushed myself too hard today, and right now I'm as sore as an old coot," he admitted with a hint of laughter in his voice. "I guess that's appropriate when I think about it, because that's actually what I've become."

"I don't agree with your premise, sir. How's George managing?"

"Somehow he has more stamina than I do, and the man's got at least twenty years on me," Jake protested. "It's just not fair."

"Are you making any more progress?" I asked, happy to talk about anything but murder.

"We're managing. How's it going with you?"

It was time to let the real world back in. After giving him a recap of our activities since Autumn had found her mother-in-law's body, I heard Jake snort when I got to the part where Chief Seaborne had tried to intimidate me into quitting. I'd left out the part where Adam had grabbed me, and I'd most likely take that bit to the grave with me. I was still afraid of how Jake would react to the news that someone had manhandled me. If I was lucky, I wouldn't bruise, so he'd never have to know what had happened.

"She had to be out of her mind to try to bully *you* of all people into backing down," Jake said.

"I'm sure she thought it was worth a shot. I kind of insulted her," I admitted, not proud of my earlier behavior.

"In what way?" he asked calmly.

"She called me the donut detective, and I retaliated by implying that she wasn't up to solving a jaywalking case, let alone a murder."

"Okay," he said.

"I had to defend my honor. You should have heard the way she said 'donut detective' to me."

"I don't know. I kind of like the ring it has to it," Jake said softly. I could tell he was trying not to laugh, which cooled my anger some as I remembered the experience. "How did you leave things with her?"

"I think she kind of admired me for standing up to her. I'm pretty sure there aren't many people around here willing to risk her wrath."

"Most likely not," he admitted. "You're not going to give up, are you?"

"What do you think?" I asked him.

"I retract the question," he said. "My offer still stands, if you want me."

I hadn't gotten to the part about finding the speaker or our plans to set out to trap whoever was trying to rattle us. It wasn't that I didn't want to share everything with my husband, but why worry him before there was anything else to report? If I knew my husband, his current state of exhaustion wouldn't matter if he thought I might be in real danger, and I couldn't risk having him drive nearly a hundred miles in his condition. "Thanks, but for the moment, we've got things covered. Autumn and I cleared the air between us, and everything's fine right now."

"She's under a great deal of stress at the moment, Suzanne," Jake reminded me softly. "Cut her some slack."

"I have," I said.

"I'm not criticizing you; you know that, right?" he asked, a hint of uncertainty in his voice.

"Of course I know it," I answered. "I'm the first to admit that sometimes I need you to keep me in check."

"Hah. I never signed up for that job, and I wouldn't take it if you held a gun to my head. You, my dear sweet wife, are a force of nature, and I know it better than anyone."

I heard the timer go off in the kitchen. "The brownies are ready," I said. "I've got to go."

"You're having brownies?" he asked, his voice dripping with envy.

"Triple chocolate," I admitted. "I'd offer to save you one, but we both know that would be an empty promise."

"At least have a bite for me," he said.

"You bet."

"Love you. Be careful."

"Right back at you," I said as we finished our call. I began to wonder the moment I put my phone away if I should have told him everything after all, but I knew that I couldn't bring myself to allow him to risk his life driving that far when he was exhausted, especially for what might turn out to be a false alarm.

It was a bad situation all the way around, but in the end, I believed that I'd made the best choice given a bad set of options.

"What do we do now?" Autumn whispered to me. Did she think the cottage had been bugged? I hadn't really considered it, but I suddenly realized that it might be at that.

Lowering my own voice as I turned on the water in the kitchen sink to a full blast, I said, "Get ready for bed, but as soon as you turn out your light, change back into jeans and a T-shirt and we'll meet back here. No lights, okay?"

"Okay," she said softly. "Do we really have to change into pjs first?" she asked me.

"If you had blinds, no, but since this place doesn't, we have to go through the motions."

"Got it," she said with a nod. "Don't forget your cast iron skillet."

"Or your pepper spray," I told her.

We went through the motions of going to bed as though someone might be watching us, and after calling out good night to Autumn, I changed into my jammies and turned off my light. In an instant I began to change back, and soon I was dressed and in the kitchen. I nearly stumbled into a chair, but I caught myself just in time. Autumn joined me a few moments later, and after putting on our jackets, we quietly crept out the back door. It squeaked slightly, and I grimaced. Had we just given ourselves away? I stood there in the darkness listening all around us for any sign that we'd been detected, but there was nothing but the usual sounds of the night. Motioning for Autumn to go ahead of me, I was happy there was a sliver of moonlight coming through the trees. It was enough to allow us to see what we were doing but not bright enough to show anyone who might be out there that we were about to join them.

"What now?" Autumn whispered after I'd slowly closed the back door of the cottage. Fortunately it didn't make a sound as I did so.

"Now we wait," I said.

"Do we just stand here?" she asked me.

"No. Let's grab the rocking chairs from the front porch and move them over into the trees where we can watch that speaker."

Autumn nodded in agreement, and after we'd positioned the chairs, we settled into watch. I was glad that both chairs had light blankets thrown over their backs. Though it was still on the edge of summer, the nights in the mountains were getting chilly. We sat in silence, but nothing happened for what felt like hours. I risked checking my watch under the blanket and was startled to find that we'd only been outside for forty-two minutes! This was going to feel like a lifetime.

"If you want to nod off for a bit, I'll keep lookout," Autumn said. "You've got to be beat."

"I am, but I don't want to leave you to watch all by yourself."

"Suzanne, it's *way* past your bedtime. By the time you're ready to wake up at your usual time, I'll be ready to sleep."

I wanted to argue with her, but I wasn't sure how long I was going to last. "Okay, but promise that you'll wake me up at the first sign of anything out of the ordinary, whether it seems important to you or not."

"I promise," she said.

I hadn't expected to fall asleep so quickly, or even at all, but my internal clock wouldn't let me force myself to stay awake. In college, I'd been able to pull all-nighters to study without consequence, but I was a long way from those days now. I fell asleep almost instantly and didn't wake back up until 2:30, my usual time on a workday.

"Thanks for the nap, Autumn." I waited a moment and then asked, "Autumn? Are you awake?"

There wasn't a sound from her except heavy breathing.

It appeared that our late-night vigil had failed after all.

Chapter 22

"I'M SO SORRY I FELL asleep," she said softly yet again.

"Don't keep beating yourself up about it," I answered. I took my phone from my pocket and opened up the flashlight app.

"Should you be doing that?" she asked me as I stood and moved to where the speaker had been haphazardly placed.

"I have a feeling it doesn't matter anymore." I used the light from my phone to check out the spot where we'd seen the speaker earlier.

Just as I suspected, it was gone.

In a normal voice, I said, "Well, at least we tried."

"Suzanne, I'm curious about something. Why didn't we hear any voices tonight?"

I thought about it a moment before answering her. "Since whoever put it here didn't have time to conceal it properly, maybe they were worried we'd investigate and see what they'd been up to. Then again, it could have been set to cut off if anyone was close by."

"Can they do that?" she asked me.

"I honestly have no idea."

"I can't believe how stupid I was, falling asleep like that," she chided herself.

"We were both exhausted," I said. "At least whoever came back to get it didn't see us."

"Why do you say that?"

"We're both still alive," I said somberly. "Come on, let's put the chairs back up on the porch and try to get a little more sleep."

She stopped in her tracks. "Do you really think that if the killer had spotted us, we'd be dead right now?"

"I don't know," I said, "but it's a possibility we have to consider, if in fact the same person who killed Cecile set that speaker up."

"Do you honestly think there's *two* of them?" she asked me incredulously.

"Whoever has been trying to make you think you're losing your mind might not be the same person who killed your mother-in-law."

"Isn't that an awfully big coincidence?" she asked me after we'd put the chairs back in place and were once again safely inside behind locked doors.

"Not really. When you think about it, it almost makes sense that it's two different people. After all, after killing Cecile, why would they still try to make you think you're going mad slowly? It's a bit subtle for someone who would take a marble rolling pin and hit your mother-in-law over the head."

"So, does that mean that *two* people are after me?" she asked.

"The truth of the matter is that Cecile's murder might not have *anything* to do with your situation," I told her.

"But it might, right?"

"Yes, it's a possibility. Listen, we're not going to do either one of us any good by missing more sleep. We can talk about it in the morning, okay?"

"Okay," she said reluctantly, "though I don't know how I'm ever going to be able to get back to sleep after that."

"Just close your eyes and see what happens," I said. "Good night. Again."

"Night," she said.

I lay in my bed trying to will sleep to come, but it was reluctant to visit. I had that problem sometimes, but when counting donuts didn't work, I'd learned a way to relax my muscles systematically, going from my toes to my scalp, and oftentimes by the time I finished the routine of tightening and then loosening muscle groups in a specific order, I was ready to sleep.

It must have worked again, because before I knew it, I was waking up.

I hadn't been in the living room five minutes when Autumn came out. "Did you manage to fall back asleep at all?" she asked me as she stifled a yawn. At least she was already dressed, as was I.

"I did. How about you?"

"I slept, but it wasn't very restful. I'd tell you my dream, but I haven't eaten anything yet."

"Do you still believe that?" I asked her with a smile.

"Sure I do. I know it's just a silly superstition, but why risk it?" She grabbed a small bite of pie we'd bought at the store and then grinned at me. "Besides, it's a perfect excuse to eat pie first thing in the morning."

"What was your dream about?"

"That we caught the person who left the speaker," she said. "We chased him through the woods, and I had just caught up to him when I grabbed his cloak and yanked it off his head."

"He was wearing a cloak?" I asked, doing my best to suppress a smile. "For that matter, it was a he?"

"It was," she said as she frowned.

"So, who was behind the cloak?"

Autumn shrugged. "I never got to see his face. That's when I woke up, but I could swear I knew who it was for one split second before I came completely awake. Does it mean anything, or did I dream that because I want to know who's been trying to drive me crazy?"

"Who knows? It could be a little bit of both," I admitted. "Should we grab a quick bite here before we start digging again?"

"I'd like to go back to the Blue Ridge Café if it's all the same to you," Autumn said.

"More of those pancakes do sound awfully good to me."

"It's not just that," she said. "I'd like to talk to Davis again. Maybe he's been able to come up with something else to help us."

As I stood, I asked, "Are you sure you're up to the scrutiny you're going to get if we go there? I'd be happy to whip up some cake donuts for us. It won't take long at all."

"As much as I'm sure I'd love them, no matter how much I've been protesting otherwise," she said with a smile, "I don't think we can pass up the opportunity to see what our only ally in town thinks."

"It's a deal," I said. "I can always make you donuts before I leave."

"I'm holding you to that," she said.

We were just heading into the café when someone called Autumn's name from behind us. It was a portly man with a mop of gray hair. He was dressed in a suit that was clearly nearing the edge of the girth it could contain, and there was a briefcase tucked under one arm that was stuffed with papers to the point that some of them were in very real danger of escaping his clutches.

"Mr. Lincoln, what can I do for you?" Autumn asked as he joined us.

"It's Carter, Autumn. Mr. Lincoln was my father," the attorney said with a smile. It was clearly a line he trotted out with some regularity. "And it's what I can do for you. I need to speak with you about Cecile Marbury's will."

"Why on earth would you need to speak with *me*?" Autumn asked.

He looked around the square and frowned. "If we could just go to my office, this won't take long." He glanced at me. "I'm sure your friend won't mind waiting for you."

"If you have something to say to me, you can say it in front of her," Autumn said firmly.

He frowned again. "And you are?"

"Suzanne Hart, donutmaker," I said.

That got a smile. "Ah, a profession I can fully endorse. Where are you based, Ms. Hart?"

"It's Suzanne," I said. "Ms. Hart is my mother, and I live in April Springs."

"Ah, very good," he said. "And if I may ask, what is your relationship with Ms. Marbury?"

"This one?" I asked as I pointed to Autumn.

"Yes, of course."

"We were roommates in college, and we're still very good friends," I answered, which Autumn acknowledged by smiling and nodding once.

"Very good. Shall we, ladies? As I said, my office isn't far."

"Of course," I said as I looked longingly back at the Blue Ridge Café and those pancakes I was craving. I was certain they'd still have some when we finished up with the attorney.

At least I hoped so.

And besides, finding out about Cecile's will was more important than breakfast.

At least that's what I told myself as we followed the attorney back to his office.

This law office was in stark contrast to Tom's workplace. It was cluttered with files and paperwork, the furniture hadn't been updated in many years, and there was an overall air of stuffiness to the place. It felt like a lived-in space and not some gallery display. "Excuse the mess," he said automatically. "My secretary is out on maternity leave, and things tend to fall apart when she has another baby."

"Does it happen often?" I asked as I studied the condition of the place.

"Oh, yes, there's nothing she enjoys more than having little ones," he said with a smile. "See that play area in the corner? If I didn't let her bring her sweet little devils to work with her when she needed to, I'd never see her at all. They're a pack of rascals, I'll tell you," he said as he smiled wistfully. It was pretty clear that he enjoyed every second of it and that he missed the kids just as much as he did his secretary.

"I don't suppose there's any reason you can't hear this, Suzanne." He then turned back to my friend. "If you're sure you want her to."

"I'm certain of it," Autumn said.

"Very well. Barring any unforeseen circumstances, once the estate has been settled, you will receive one million dollars in cash when all is said and done."

That certainly caught Autumn off guard. "Excuse me? Are you quite sure about that?"

"Mrs. Marbury was most specific," he said.

"When did she make that bequest?" I asked.

He didn't even have to consult his notes. "Three weeks ago."

"*After* I moved out?" she asked him.

"I believe that was what motivated her to change her will," he said. "She wanted to be certain that you were taken care of."

"What would happen to the bequest if Autumn and Jeff divorced?" I asked on a hunch.

He looked startled by the question. "How did you know about that clause?"

"Know what?" she asked him.

"Were you and your husband to divorce, you would receive nothing. I'm not sure if that million was to be an incentive for you to stay married or not, but she insisted on it, and I wasn't in any position to argue her out of it. My father was her father's attorney, and she kept me on as an homage to both men, but I knew how close I was to being replaced every time she came into my office."

"So, let's say Autumn and Jeff did divorce," I said. "What would happen to that money? Would it be divided equally between the two brothers, by any chance?"

"No, as a matter of fact, it would all go to Jefferson," he said.

"What about Adam?"

He frowned a moment and then said, "I really shouldn't be discussing this with you."

"Carter, we both know that it's going to be public knowledge soon enough. Are you sure you can't tell us anything?"

"I'm sorry," he said, and then he pushed the papers toward us. "Did you two hear that?"

"What? I didn't hear anything," Autumn said.

I had a feeling what he was doing. "You know, I believe I heard something, too," I said.

"I'd better go check outside. We've had some cars broken into around here lately. I shouldn't be gone more than three minutes," he said as he stood and left us.

The moment the door closed, I flipped the document in question around and started scanning it.

"Suzanne, should you be doing that?" Autumn asked me. "You heard what he said."

"Autumn, he practically invited us to read it. Wow," I said as I looked up and put the will back where it belonged.

"What did it say?"

I was about to tell her when the door opened again. Soon Carter was back behind his desk. "Again, I'm sorry I can't be of more help to you."

"It's fine," I said quickly. "We understand completely."

"Is that all?" Autumn asked.

"For now," Carter acknowledged.

We got up and headed for the door, but before we could get there, he said, "There's one more thing, Mrs. Marbury."

"What's that?" she stopped and asked.

"Nothing will be settled until whoever killed Cecile Marbury is caught and convicted. I'm sorry, but there's nothing that can be done about that. The court needs to be certain that whoever killed her doesn't profit from the crime."

Autumn was about to say something when I headed her off. "She understands."

As we were leaving, he said, "I'm not saying that's what I believe to be the case. I'm just telling you how it must play out officially."

"Thanks again," I said, and then I got Autumn out of there.

As we walked back toward the café, Autumn stopped me and asked, "What exactly was in that will?"

"Adam gets an allowance for the rest of his natural life, but Jeff inherits the bulk of the estate," I said. "She actually cut her older son out of the will, but there are a few conditions that might come into play."

"What are those?"

"If you and your husband divorce, and then if something happens to Jeff, Adam gets everything."

Chapter 23

"DOES THAT MEAN THAT *he's* behind everything that's been happening to me? He killed his own mother for *money*?" She said it with such disdain, so much contempt, but I knew it had happened before and would just as surely happen again. Some people were driven so hard by their lust for money that everything else fell by the wayside.

"Hang on. I know that it looks bad for Adam, but it doesn't necessarily mean that he killed Cecile. Let me remind you that we have other suspects, too."

"Do you still think that Jeff could have done it?" she asked me, clearly outraged by the very thought of it.

"Autumn, that will gives him every reason to want to see his mother dead," I told her, "whether you like it or not."

"If that's true, why would he kill her *before* we got divorced?" she asked.

"That's a good point. He stands to lose a million dollars as things stand right now. For that matter, why would Adam do it?" I countered.

"So we don't know any more than we did last night?" she asked me, the pain clear in her question.

"I wouldn't say that," I replied. "The more information we have, the better." I looked down the road near the café and saw Annie talking to someone who was sitting in his car. She was laughing at something he said, and she had her hand on his arm, stroking it lightly. "Is that Annie Greenway? Who is that she's talking to?"

"That would be my husband," Autumn said coolly as she started toward the car.

The moment Annie saw us heading her way, she started walking quickly in the opposite direction. It was pretty clear to me that Autumn wanted to go after her, but Jeff got out of the car and headed her off before I could.

"It's not what it looks like," Jeff said quickly.

"What, that we're not even divorced yet and you're already flirting with another woman?" Autumn asked him angrily.

"I didn't encourage it," Jeff said.

"Do you deny that she's been throwing herself at you even before we got married? Why *did* you marry me instead of her?" Autumn asked him. "Clearly she's better suited to be a Marbury than I ever was."

"The problem was that I never loved *her*," Jeff said. "At least not the way I love you. I know that I've been a fool these past few days, but it doesn't change the way I feel about you. When are you coming back home, Autumn? I need you now, more than ever."

"I was under the impression that you thought I might have killed your mother," she said softly.

"That was Adam. I *never* said it."

"You didn't defend me, though," she said fiercely.

"I was in shock! I'd just lost my mother," he protested. "I love you, Autumn, and I want you in my life. What can I do to make things right between us again?"

"Throw your brother out of the house, for starters," she said.

"He's gone as soon as I can give him the news," Jeff said. "What else?"

Autumn looked shocked by his ready agreement. "Do you mean that?"

"I do," he said.

"How about the house? I don't think I can ever live there again," she said, clearly wavering.

"I can't either, especially after what happened to my mother. We'll sell it, so you don't ever have to step foot in it again," Jeff said. "We can buy another place together, or I can move in with you at the cottage, if you'll let me. I'd live in a tent if it meant that I could be with you again."

"I don't know," she said, clearly caught off guard by his change of attitude. "Why the sudden change of heart?"

"Losing my mother made me realize that I can't lose you, too," he said. "Do you want me to beg? Because I will, if that's what it takes." He followed through on his offer by getting down on his knees in front of her. "I'm sorry. I was wrong. About so many things. Please forgive me."

"Get up, Jeff," she said as she tugged at her estranged husband's arm. "You're making a scene."

"I don't care," he said, and I believed him.

"By the way, she's not going crazy. There really were voices," I said. "I heard them, too, and this morning we found a speaker that had been planted outside our windows."

"Where is it?" he asked.

It was a reasonable question. Unfortunately, I didn't have a good answer for him. "Whoever planted it came back and got it without us seeing them," I said, "but it was there."

"I believe you," he said as he finally stood. "Tell me what to do, Autumn."

"Let me think about it," she said.

Did I catch a glimmer of hope cross his expression? "Really? It's at least a possibility?"

"Really," she said with a smile.

Without invitation, he leaned forward and hugged her. It surprised both of us, but what startled me even more was that she didn't pull away. "A possibility, I said," she added softly.

"I'll take whatever I can get," he said as he pulled away.

It was a sweet scene, the first step to a possible reconciliation, when it was interrupted by someone shouting at Autumn as he hurried forward.

Evidently I hadn't been the only one to witness the reunion.

Lee Graham was hurrying toward us, and he didn't look at all happy about the situation.

"Don't get caught up in his lies, Autumn," Lee said fiercely when he got to us.

I had to give Jeff credit. He was forty pounds heavier and at least fifteen years older than the strapping young handyman, but he didn't flinch. "Stay out of this, Lee. It's between Autumn and me."

"He's just using you," Lee said. "Can't you see that?"

"Lee, he's my husband!" Autumn said fiercely. "*Nothing* is going to happen between us, especially after yesterday."

She'd clearly meant the death of Cecile, but he interpreted it to be something else. A look of guilt crossed his face that couldn't be denied. The handyman had dropped his mask for just a moment, and I'd seen it. He was terrified about something, so I played my hunch. "It's all over. We saw you last night," I said coldly. Autumn was about to say something, so I had to stop her before Lee spoke. "Let him talk. He deserves the right to explain himself."

Autumn nodded, still clearly not understanding what was really going on, when Lee said, "You don't understand. I had to do it."

"Really?" I asked. "You *had* to?"

"Sure, maybe Adam paid me, but it was what I wanted anyway."

"*You* killed my mother?" Jeff asked as he grabbed the younger man's shirt and nearly lifted him off the ground.

"What? No!" he shouted as he broke Jeff Marbury's grip. "Of course not! I set up the speaker at the cottage last night and then took it away after a few hours, just like I did every night at your house, but I didn't have anything to do with killing Mrs. Marbury! I liked her. Why would I kill her?"

"Hold on a second," Autumn said. "*You* were the one trying to drive me crazy? I thought you cared about me."

"I didn't think it would hit you so hard," Lee explained. "And besides, I thought it might pry you free from *him*," he said as he stepped back from his attacker.

"Did you loosen that rail and try to drop that gargoyle on me, too?" she asked him coldly.

"The gargoyle was me," he admitted. "I purposely missed you by a mile! It was just meant to scare you enough so that you'd leave Jeff."

"But you didn't have anything to do with the fence?" I asked.

"I didn't touch it. If anyone did it, it was Adam," he said. "You've got to believe me, Autumn. It's not too late for us."

She gave him the iciest stare I'd ever seen in my life. "You're the one who has lost his mind. I don't ever want to see you again. Do you understand?"

He looked shattered by the news. "Just give me a chance to make things right with you," he protested.

"If you don't leave this second, I'm calling the police and telling them what you did," Autumn said.

"You should call them anyway," Jeff protested.

"Stay out of this, Jefferson. I'm handling it," she told him firmly, and he held up his hands and took a few steps backward. It was great seeing that my old friend was back in full force.

"Understood," he said.

"Go, Lee. Now. I mean it." Her voice was devoid of all emotion. I think the fact that she wasn't screaming at him threw him off. Hanging his head, the handyman walked away, clearly a beaten man.

"I still can't believe it," Autumn said once he was gone.

"What, that Lee tried to drive you away from me, or that Adam paid him to do it? Why would he even *do* something like that?"

"You haven't spoken with Carter Lincoln yet, have you?" I asked him.

"No, he's been calling me ever since he found out that my mother died, but I haven't wanted to speak with him," Jeff admitted. He turned to Autumn. "Why, have you?"

"He tracked us down twenty minutes ago," she admitted. "Jeff, your mother left me a million dollars, but only on the condition that we stay together. Adam had incentive to break us up, but that's not all."

"There's more? What else could there be?" he asked. "I'm going to kill him when I get my hands on my dear brother."

"I'm afraid that's the plan he has in store for you," I said. "If you two split up and then *you* die, he gets everything."

Chapter 24

"WHAT ARE YOU TALKING about? I'm pretty sure that Henry Charleston killed my mother," Jeff said. "I'm glad you called me last night, Autumn," he told his wife. "I had the auditors move in before he could destroy the evidence. It's true, he's been stealing from my mother for years, but evidently she finally found out about it. He confessed everything to the police this morning. That's why I came here looking for you. I went by the cottage, but you were already gone."

"He actually confessed to killing Cecile?" I asked him.

"No, just to embezzling from her, but the police chief was pretty sure he'd admit to killing my mother before long. It's just a matter of time before it's all wrapped up."

"I don't think so," I said, something nagging at my mind.

"Do you still think Adam did it?" he asked me. "He might be lowlife scum, but why would he kill our mother while Autumn and I were still married? It doesn't make sense."

"No, it doesn't," I admitted, not mentioning the fact that it cleared him as well. If he had killed Cecile for the money, it would only make sense if it had happened *after* he and Autumn were divorced, which was clearly a possibility, considering where they had been heading. As things stood now, he'd have to share *everything* with her, despite his mother's bequest.

So who did that leave?

And then the last puzzle piece fell into place.

We needed to find Annie Greenway, and we needed to find her fast.

"Why Annie?" Autumn asked as we all got into Jeff's car.

"She's the only one who still makes sense," I explained. "Do you happen to know where she lives?" I asked Jeff.

"Sure," he admitted.

"Then drive, and don't stop for any red lights," I ordered. Autumn had taken the front passenger seat, and I was sitting in back.

"Talk to us, Suzanne," she said.

"Okay, let's eliminate our suspects. If Adam did it for the money, or Jeff..."

"He didn't do it," she said firmly before he could defend himself. That seemed to please him, but we didn't have time for any side trips.

"Or Jeff," I continued, "then the order of events was all wrong. Lee wouldn't kill her because his fight was with Jeff, not his mother. While it's true that Charleston may have had motive aplenty, he knew he was caught from the moment folks started to wonder about him, and that was quite a while before Cecile was murdered. Remember, Davis told us people around town have been speculating about his trustworthiness for weeks now. That leaves Annie, and Davis also told us that she had a very public fight with Cecile a few days before she was murdered. If she wanted your mother's approval, Jeff, and she didn't get it, she might resort to murder just to get another obstacle out of the way."

"I can't believe it," Jeff said. "That would make her some kind of psychopath, wouldn't it?"

"People have killed for worse reasons than that," I told him. "Autumn said it herself. The woman's been obsessed with you for years. If your mother stood between the two of you, in her mind it might have been the next logical step."

"Maybe, but murder?"

"I know that it might be a stretch, but that's why we're going there first to talk to her before we call the police," I said. "I have a feeling we can break her, if you're there with us. What do you say?"

"If it will help solve my mother's murder, then I'm in," he said as he reached across the seat and took his wife's hand in his.

The funny thing was, Autumn didn't pull away.

When we got to Annie's house, I told them, "Stay back and let me handle this."

Something told me to peek in the window before I rang the bell, and wow, was I ever glad that I did. It might have been the sound of Annie's voice or the whimpering I heard in the background, but something was surely amiss.

Through the open screen window, I could see Adam tied to a chair, his mouth covered with duct tape and one arm and both legs bound with it as well. He was writing something with his free hand, taking dictation really, as Annie stood over him, a knife just a bare inch from his throat.

Apparently we'd gotten there just in time.

Or was it possible that we were already too late?

Chapter 25

"WALK BACK TO THE OTHER side of the car and call the police," I told Autumn quietly. "Annie has Adam tied up in there, and she's got a knife at his throat."

"What are you going to do?" Autumn asked me softly as she pulled out her phone.

"I'm going to try to stop her," I said.

"Using what?" she asked. "Your cast iron pan is back at the cottage. Take this," she said as she grabbed the pepper spray from her purse.

"I'm coming with you," Jeff said to me.

"You don't have to risk it," I told him.

"He's my brother, even if he is a snake. What's the plan?" He seemed ready if not eager to get involved, and the truth was that I could use the backup. If the situation hadn't been so dire, I would have waited for the police, but I was afraid that Adam would be dead by then. I had no love for the man, but even he deserved better than dying at this crazy woman's hand.

"Go around back and throw something heavy through a window or that glass sliding door," I said as I noticed it behind Annie and Adam.

"What are you going to do?"

"When she turns around, I'm going to jump through the window screen and rush her," I said.

"What if it doesn't work?" he asked me, hesitating.

"It is what it is. I know one thing, though. If we do nothing, he's going to die, and I don't want that on my conscience. Do you?" I stared at him for two full seconds before he shook his head.

"No, let's do this."

Jeff hurried around back, and I tried to see if I could get through the screen and to Annie before she could attack Adam, or Jeff either, for that matter.

I decided I had a few seconds, so I walked to the front door, trying to stay out of sight as I did so. Was there any chance it was unlocked?

It was! I was stunned when the doorknob turned in my hand! It was certainly going to be a lot easier than jumping through a screened window, getting my balance, and attacking this lunatic of a woman who was armed with a knife.

All I had was pepper spray. I looked around the porch and saw a small ornamental flag on a thin metal pole. The flag was waving in the breeze, and the rod holding it didn't look very strong, but it was better than nothing. I pulled the stake out of the ground and bunched the flag up as a handle when I heard something crash through the glass at the back of the house.

I was fully expecting to see Annie rushing toward the back when I burst into the house, but she hadn't moved a muscle.

The knife was still poised at Adam's throat, and she looked at me as though she'd been expecting me all along.

"Come in, Suzanne. You should get whoever is helping you to come in, too. We'll make it a party." There wasn't a hint of disturbance in her voice, something that chilled me more than a homicidal rant would have accomplished.

This was one seriously unbalanced woman we were dealing with, and evidently she wasn't about to give up until at least some of us were dead.

"She knows. You might as well come in," I called out as I walked into the house.

"Drop that," Annie said as she gestured to the flag holder in my hands.

I complied, and she actually smiled at me. "That's a good girl." Her knife never wavered for a moment from Adam's throat, and I could see by the look in his eyes that he was terrified.

I couldn't blame him. We'd come to rescue him, but instead, now we were all in the middle of a bad situation that I'd somehow found a way to make worse.

Chapter 26

"WHAT'S GOING ON HERE, Annie?" Jeff asked her as he walked into the room from the back of the house.

"Jeff? What are you doing here?" she asked incredulously.

"I came to talk to you," he said. "Annie, maybe we can work things out."

He was trying to calm her down, and from the way the knife dipped slowly, I knew that it just might work. I had to be ready with the spray, stuffed in my pocket, if the opportunity presented itself, though. I was still eight steps from her, and so was Jeff. If I tried to spray her now, I'd surely get Adam, but that was the least of my worries. I needed a solid four steps before I could be sure to get it into her eyes at all, and for that, I needed Jeff to keep on talking.

"It's too late for us," she said bitterly. "You said so yourself not an hour ago." The knife moved closer to Adam's neck, and I saw him stiffen as the blade lightly touched the skin. A small trickle of blood danced down his neck from the wound, and he grunted from the pain.

"I may have been hasty," he said. "We should at least talk about it. You should know that I forgive you."

"For kidnapping Adam? I've done much worse than that," she admitted. "Cecile wouldn't give me her blessing. She said that she'd come to realize that you belonged with Autumn. I lost my mind, Jeff. I shoved her, I admit that much, but she tripped and hit her head."

"On a rolling pin?" I asked her. I should have kept my mouth shut, but I couldn't let her get away with the delusional scenario she was describing.

"It was all one big accident, but I can't undo any of it now," she said. "Adam was just finishing up his suicide note and confession, but that's not going to do us any good now, is it? I've got to come up with a new plan."

"Annie, I'll go to the police with you. We'll tell them what happened, that it was all an accident," Jeff said.

As she turned to look at him, I took two steps forward. She didn't notice, but I was committed. The second she turned around to look at me again, I'd have to strike.

Jeff said, "We can still be together."

"But you don't love me," she said, tears starting to track down her cheeks. "You told me so yourself."

Before Jeff could say a word, the front door opened, and Autumn rushed in, brandishing a tire iron and screaming her head off. I leapt forward and sprayed Annie before Autumn could get to her. The killer dropped the knife, and I picked it up as Jeff pinned her arms from behind.

She seemed to melt back into his embrace, as though it had been her plan all along.

I ripped the duct tape from Adam's mouth, and as I was working on freeing his one arm and both legs, Autumn stood over him and slapped his face viciously. "You tried to make me think that I'd lost my mind."

The recent captive started weeping openly, either from the accusation or the trauma he'd suffered so recently. "They loved you more than they loved me," he whimpered. "You had to go."

"So you could kill Jeff and get everything?" she asked him, quivering where she stood, filled with rage.

"What? No! I never wanted that! I just wanted them to love me again."

Autumn looked at him with open contempt. "I feel sorry for you," she said as Chief Seaborne arrived and took custody of Annie from Jeff.

I could swear the vicious killer resented the presence of the police, and the sudden absence of Jeff's arms around her, more than she did being found out.

After Annie was led away, Jeff told his brother, "I don't want to know you anymore. You need to leave, and don't ever come back."

Adam asked chokingly, "Mother's funeral is in two days. Can I at least stay for that? I'm so sorry. Can you both ever forgive me?"

"No," Jeff said firmly.

Autumn evidently had a change of heart. "Jeff."

He turned to her, and she shrugged slightly. "Let him stay, at least for the funeral."

Jeff took that in and mulled it over before he answered. "Fine, but remember this, Adam. It's because of Autumn that you are staying, not because of me."

"I understand. Give me a chance, and I'll make it up to you both," Adam said.

"Let's see how the next few days go," Autumn said as the paramedics arrived. They started to treat Adam's wound when Chief Seaborne came back in.

"Ms. Hart, may I have a moment?"

"Of course," I said. I didn't want to get in the middle of the family discussion anyway. Either they'd all work it out or not, but at that point, it was none of my business. Whatever Autumn decided to do was fine by me now. She'd found her spirit again, and I trusted her to do what was best for her and her family.

"I just wanted to say that I'm sorry I didn't trust you," the chief said right out of the gate. "I was wrong."

"It's okay," I said. "This entire case turned out to be one big mess. Just about everyone involved *but* Jeff ended up doing something wrong."

"But you managed to figure it all out before I did," she admitted graciously.

"Once I saw the right way to attack the problem, it was the only way that it all made sense. Annie was the *only* one who didn't have a monetary motive," I said. "The truth is that I never really seriously considered Lee, and everyone else, from Jeff to Adam to Charleston, all had reasons to want Cecile to be alive. Only Annie had a reason to want her dead, so she could get close to Jeff. I have a feeling if we hadn't figured this out and Jeff and Autumn really did reconcile, *she* would have been Annie's next victim."

"You're probably right," she said as she extended her hand, which I shook. "No hard feelings?"

"None at all," I said.

"When you see your husband next, tell him I said hello," she said as she headed for her squad car, where Annie was waiting patiently in back as though she was in a limo and not being taken into custody.

"I'll do that," I said.

Chapter 27

"ARE YOU *sure* you can't stay any longer?" Autumn asked as she hugged me good-bye.

"I'm sorry, but I need to get home to my husband and my own family," I explained. "I have a feeling you'll be just fine without me."

"I couldn't have made it through this without you," she said as she hugged me even harder. "You know that, don't you?"

"I'm just happy I could help. Are you going to be okay?"

"Yes, I believe I will be, now."

I couldn't help myself. I had to know. "How do things stand between you and Jeff?"

"He's taking me out on a date the day after the funeral," she said. "I'm not letting him move in just yet, but I'm not willing to write my marriage off, either."

"That sounds like a good plan to me," I said. "What about Adam?"

"He's staying on a trial basis. Jeff is still ready to kill him, but he's all the family he has left, so I'm trying to get him to at least give him another chance."

"That's not quite true though, is it?"

"What do you mean?" she asked me.

"He's still got you."

As I drove back home, I found my thoughts drifting to my mother, my husband, and all of my friends. Momma was rich, apparently even richer than I'd realized, but she was worth so much more to me alive than she would ever be dead. I knew that I wouldn't have her forever, but I'd take every day I could get.

Jake was a treasure, too. He gave me exactly the right amount of space I needed to lead my own life and still be a very important part of it as well. I was lucky to have him, and I knew it. To be fair, he said the same thing about me, but wasn't that what *everyone* in a healthy and strong marriage said?

I was happy to be going home, and not just to April Springs.

Home to me was wherever the people I loved were.

And having that made me richer than anybody else in the world.

In the end, love was the only currency that I cared about.

RECIPES

Hot Cocoa Treats

A blast from the past that I've loved since first stumbling onto it years ago, no matter the season. For an extra blast, make these and serve them with piping-hot cups of cocoa for a double whammy you won't soon forget!

Ingredients

Dry

1 cup bread flour (unbleached all-purpose flour can be used as well)

1/2 cup hot chocolate mix (a store-bought powder works fine)

1 teaspoon baking powder

1/4 teaspoon baking soda

1/4 teaspoon nutmeg

1/4 teaspoon cinnamon

1/8 teaspoon salt

Wet

1 egg, beaten

1/2 cup chocolate milk (2% or whole preferred)

3 tablespoons butter, melted

1/2 cup granulated sugar

1 teaspoon vanilla extract

Directions

In a large bowl, combine the dry ingredients (flour, hot chocolate mix, baking powder, baking soda, nutmeg, cinnamon, and salt) and sift together. In a separate bowl, combine the wet ingredients (beaten egg, chocolate milk, butter, sugar, and vanilla). Slowly add the wet mix to the dry mix, stirring until it's all incorporated, but don't overmix.

Bake in the oven at 350°F for 10 to 15 minutes in cupcake trays or small donut molds. I bought a dedicated donut baker that sits on my countertop, and I absolutely love it. It's easy to use, reliable, not expensive at all, and makes perfect donuts every time. These donuts usually take 6 to 7 minutes to make.

Once the donuts are finished, remove them to a cooling rack. After they cool just a bit, they can be covered with chocolate icing or a chocolate glaze with chocolate sprinkles for an extra jolt, but actually, they are good enough to eat as they come out of the oven.

Makes 5 to 9 donuts, depending on baking method

The Easiest Donut You'll Ever Make

I'm almost embarrassed to admit how often I've made these in the past. They are so easy and delicious that when I'm feeling ultra lazy, these are my go-to treats. Try them yourself, and you'll see what I mean!

Ingredients

1 can biscuit dough (I like the sourdough recipe)

Directions

Preheat canola oil to 375°F.

Remove biscuit dough from container, then cut into desired shapes.

Add to oil, turning once after 2 minutes.

Drain on paper towels, then eat plain or with confectioners' sugar or powdered chocolate.

Makes 4 to 8 donuts

Lemon Perfection Donuts

Lemon is one of my favorite flavors in the world, and making these just reinforces that feeling. When you want a taste of spring, no matter what the season, give these delights a try!

Ingredients

1 1/2 cups all-purpose flour

1 teaspoon baking soda

4 teaspoons confectioners' sugar

Dash of salt

1 egg, beaten

1/4 cup milk (whole or 2%)

1/4 cup lemonade (sweetened)

2 teaspoons lemon juice

Lemon zest (one lemon)

Four crushed lemon candies, about 1 tablespoon (entirely optional)

Canola oil, enough to submerge the donuts

Directions

Heat enough canola oil to fry your treats to 365°F.

While the oil is heating, in a medium-sized bowl, sift the flour, baking soda, confectioners' sugar, and salt together. Set it aside, and in a larger bowl, beat the egg, then add the milk, lemonade, lemon juice, and lemon zest. Stir to combine the ingredients, then slowly add the dry mix to the wet, stirring thoroughly as you go. Now is the time to mix in the candies in the batter if you choose to go that route. Use two tablespoons, one to scoop the batter and the other to slide it off into the oil once it comes to temperature. Cook each drop for 2 to 3 minutes until golden brown, and then remove from the oil and place on a paper towel. A dusting of confectioners' sugar is optional, but we always do it at my house!

Makes approximately 12 lemon drop donuts

If you enjoy Jessica Beck Mysteries and you would like to be notified when the next book is being released, please visit our website at jessicabeckmysteries.net for valuable information about Jessica's books, and sign up for her new-releases-only mail blast.

Your email address will not be shared, sold, bartered, traded, broadcast, or disclosed in any way. There will be no spam from us, just a friendly reminder when the latest book is being released, and of course, you can drop out at any time.

Other Books by Jessica Beck

The Donut Mysteries
Glazed Murder
Fatally Frosted
Sinister Sprinkles
Evil Éclairs
Tragic Toppings
Killer Crullers
Drop Dead Chocolate
Powdered Peril
Illegally Iced
Deadly Donuts
Assault and Batter
Sweet Suspects
Deep Fried Homicide
Custard Crime
Lemon Larceny
Bad Bites
Old Fashioned Crooks
Dangerous Dough
Troubled Treats
Sugar Coated Sins
Criminal Crumbs
Vanilla Vices
Raspberry Revenge
Fugitive Filling
Devil's Food Defense
Pumpkin Pleas
Floured Felonies
Mixed Malice

Tasty Trials
Baked Books
Cranberry Crimes
Boston Cream Bribes
Cherry Filled Charges
Scary Sweets
Cocoa Crush
Pastry Penalties
Apple Stuffed Alibies
Perjury Proof
Caramel Canvas
Dark Drizzles
Counterfeit Confections
Measured Mayhem
The Classic Diner Mysteries
A Chili Death
A Deadly Beef
A Killer Cake
A Baked Ham
A Bad Egg
A Real Pickle
A Burned Biscuit
The Ghost Cat Cozy Mysteries
Ghost Cat: Midnight Paws
Ghost Cat 2: Bid for Midnight
The Cast Iron Cooking Mysteries
Cast Iron Will
Cast Iron Conviction
Cast Iron Alibi
Cast Iron Motive
Cast Iron Suspicion
Nonfiction

The Donut Mysteries Cookbook

Made in the USA
Middletown, DE
26 July 2019